FORGED IN DARKNESS

FORGE BROTHERS SECURITY
BOOK 0.5

KENDRA WARDEN

CHAPTER
ONE

LAUREN

Lauren Ortega stared down at the bubbles in the kitchen sink.

She wanted to pick up the sponge and continue scrubbing, but her hands refused to obey.

"After this job, you can take a break for a while, baby. I promise," Cody was saying behind her, his fingers resting upon the strip of exposed skin at her waist. She could feel him breathing against her neck, his words sweet and gentle.

It was a promise that she knew he wouldn't keep.

"Coke or pot?" she asked, turning to face him without bothering to dry her hands on the ratty old towel hanging on the cabinet door.

Cody shook his head, his dark curls falling into his brown eyes. "Fentanyl."

She sucked in a breath.

"One job. A couple of weeks out. Local," he added quickly. "Enough cash to set us up for the next year, maybe more."

He didn't quite meet her eyes as he spoke, but she could guess what he was leaving out.

Unlike the small-scale mule work she'd done before, this job would demand she transport a large quantity of drugs.

"Would I have to cross the border at Juárez?" she asked, trying to keep her voice from shaking. Thanks to her own half-Mexican heritage, she'd be better able to fit in than most of the members of the largely white Iron Prophets gang.

"No, princess," Cody murmured, pulling her more tightly toward him. "All we're doing is picking it up for the final leg of the trip. All stateside."

Despite her frustration about what he was asking her, she couldn't help but to find comfort in his familiar embrace.

Ever since high school, she'd been his ride or die, and he'd been hers. Aside from her *abuelita*, who she rarely saw these days, her boyfriend was the one person who really loved her.

Lauren tucked a few strands of dark hair behind her ear, watching as he wiped a lingering bubble of dish soap from her forearm.

She wanted to say yes, and to make him happy, but she couldn't go in blind. She'd narrowly avoided prison on two separate occasions already, and when it came to big-time drug trafficking, the threats posed by law enforcement were the least of her worries.

"Is it cartel product?" she asked, hating the note of desperation and fear that she heard in her own voice.

Cody didn't say anything for a long moment, but finally, he nodded.

"They're working with a new manufacturer. Solid guys, clean chemistry, and most importantly, the consistent production that the Iron Prophets need if we're going to run El Paso. It's a big step up for all of us."

She looked around their small apartment as she tried to think of what to say, taking in the water-damaged corner of the living room ceiling, the missing handles on the kitchen cupboards, and the lingering smell of cigarette smoke that her scented candles could never quite vanquish.

It wasn't much, and she dreamed of something better, just like her boyfriend did, but that didn't mean she was willing to take part in a deal with El Pez and his men. She knew what they were capable of, and the drug business was never simple. Allies could become enemies in a heartbeat, and she had no interest in being left with the bag if things imploded.

"We talked about this, baby," she said carefully. "I'm not running cartel drugs. You need to get someone else."

Cody's hands fell away from her waist in an instant as anger flashed behind his eyes. She forced herself not to look away. No matter how much she tried to soften the blow, telling him no was always a risk.

"Who else?" he spat, raking a hand through his dark hair. "Who else, Lauren? Me, Dez, everyone has a record. It's not like we can trust just any of the guys."

"I know that, but—"

"But what? You keep your little button nose clean, and when it comes time to put your empty rap sheet to use, you're too good for us?"

He took a couple of steps toward her, and she found herself inching back without thinking.

No. She had to hold her ground. Cody's temper scared her, but she was more afraid of the cartel, by a long shot. They'd had this argument before. He'd promised that she could stick to street level dealing with known buyers and the occasional low-quantity carry of cocaine or marijuana.

"I'm not too good for anybody," Lauren said, crossing her arms over the front of her v-neck crop top. "But we agreed. It's my life on the line—"

Cody moved forward until his face was mere inches from her own, his dark eyes filled with rage.

She flinched, waiting for him to slap her, but the pain never came.

He shrunk back a little, his voice low and deathly calm.

"It's not just about you, princess. Family comes first.

3

Before your life, before mine, before anything. The Iron Prophets will protect you, but you need to show your loyalty in return. It's time you learned that."

She didn't dare to do anything but nod as he turned and grabbed his wallet, his gun, and a pack of cigarettes off of the messy coffee table.

"I have to work."

Without another word, he left the apartment, slamming the door behind him and leaving her alone in the silence.

Lauren let the tears she'd been holding back fall as she scrubbed at the old plastic plates and gas station coffee mugs. The water in the sink was no longer warm, but she didn't care. None of it mattered now.

Even as the longtime girlfriend of one of the highest ranking members of the gang, she had no rights, no voice, and no say in her own life.

To the men of the Iron Prophets, women were nothing but tools to be used.

They were maids to keep their cheap apartments clean, babysitters for children they didn't want to take any time to help raise, and dealers and thieves for the jobs that the men couldn't or wouldn't do.

Most of all, they were bodies, especially while they were young and pretty enough.

Lauren was twenty-seven now, and she'd been lucky enough to pay her dues so far by keeping herself in shape, doing her hair and makeup well, and giving Cody whatever he wanted, whenever he wanted it. A lot of the younger girls, especially ones who didn't have a steady boyfriend or husband in the gang, ended up as prostitutes.

They were protected by Iron Prophet pimps, and in return, they passed back a heavy percentage of their earnings.

If Lauren lost her man, she knew, she'd probably end up as one of them. She still had quite a few marketable years left. Cody ran most of the dealer crews on this side of El

Paso, and he wouldn't let her stay in the drug business if she left him.

She tossed a mac-and-cheese-coated pot into the sink, sending lukewarm water rollicking across the cheap laminate countertop.

She let out a curse.

What did loyalty matter any more? She was trapped. Either she risked her freedom and her life dealing with the cartel, or she risked her freedom and her life turning tricks on the street.

She was done.

And if she didn't find a way out now, she never would.

She left the dishes in the sink and marched toward the bedroom, ignoring the basket of laundry that still waited to be folded and the makeup products that cluttered the top of their dresser. She'd deal with her domestic responsibilities later.

She had a phone call to make before she lost her nerve.

REILLY

"Hello? Reilly? The butter?"

Reilly snapped to attention at the sound of his uncle Gabriel's voice, letting his forkful of mashed potatoes rest against the side of his plate. He'd eaten nearly half of his steak dinner without really tasting it.

"Right, sorry," he said, picking up the ceramic butter dish and a knife and passing it across the wide table.

"Daydreaming about a crazy week ahead for Forge Brothers Security?" Gabriel Sr. asked, buttering a roll as his bright blue eyes searched Reilly's face.

"You know it."

"For all of my boys, or just you?"

Reilly paused.

He wanted to tell his uncle that the reason his five sons

5

weren't here for Sunday dinner was because they were unavoidably busy with work, but his faith did not permit him to lie. Not even to spare the feelings of the man who had raised him as his own ever since the death of his parents when he was a child.

"We're all as busy as ever," he said carefully. "The job never really ends when you work for yourself."

His uncle settled back in his chair, pushing aside his own finished plate.

Reilly still half-expected his aunt Mary to come and gather up the dishes. Even after she'd been gone for nearly eight years, her presence seemed to permeate every inch of the tidy farmhouse, especially the dining room where they now sat.

His uncle had never changed her decor, and he doubted he ever would, even if the rustic wooden signs and tasteful greenery eventually became as dated as puke-colored shag rugs from the 1970s.

For Gabriel Forge Sr., traditions endured.

"Ain't that the truth," he said, giving a low chuckle. "And no, before you ask, I'm still not retiring."

"Wasn't going to say a word," Reilly said, grinning.

His uncle owned a massive agricultural company called Forge & Sons, which sold everything from farm equipment to fertilizer. Despite the fact that the titular "Sons" had run off to start their own private security firm, the old man had kept the name of the company as it was.

In the past few years, Reilly had finally managed to convince him to bring in some outside management for day to day operations, but his uncle still held on to hope that one day, his sons and his nephew would take on a more direct role in running the original Forge family business.

In the meantime, he remained stubbornly at the helm.

"It's too quiet here with just the two of us," his uncle said. "But I'm glad you came."

Reilly felt a twinge of sadness at the resignation in the older man's voice.

Though all of the men remained civil with one another, there had been tension in the family ever since his oldest cousin, Gabriel Jr., had founded Forge Brothers Security five years prior.

He and his brothers really were working a lot, but they could still put in an effort to be around more.

"Me too," Reilly said, finishing the final bites of his own steak and reaching for his iced tea.

"Well," Gabe Sr. said, getting to his feet and taking his own drink with him, "whenever I got too busy with the business on a Sunday, Mary would always remind me that God honors us when we honor His day."

Reilly nodded. "Ben and Cameron were at church with me today."

"That's good to hear," his uncle said as the two of them made their way into the living room and settled into worn leather armchairs in front of the fireplace. The late August heat didn't permit an actual fire, but Reilly still appreciated the ambiance.

He enjoyed being home. His bachelor condo in downtown San Antonio just wasn't the same.

"Gabe promised to come with us next week," he added.

"Good."

Neither he nor his uncle would give voice to what the other was thinking, but they knew. Gabriel Jr. hadn't cut himself off from their faith entirely, but it was something he fit in at the margins of his life rather than in the center of it. And as the head of the company, his margins of time and energy seemed to be becoming slimmer with each passing year.

"If you can't get my boys over here, maybe you need to try something else," his uncle suggested, his bright blue eyes twinkling as he brought his iced tea to his lips.

"Such as?"

"Bring home a nice woman for Sunday supper. If I like her, then you can get married and bring home some grandbabies. Sure would liven up the place."

Reilly shook his head, chuckling.

"I may be able to make time for the Lord, but I don't think a wife is going to be happy spending time with her husband one day a week."

His uncle raised his hands in defeat. "Fine, fine. Just think about it. You're not getting any younger."

"You're one to talk," Reilly joked. "But I will. In a couple of years. Maybe."

CHAPTER
TWO

LAUREN

Lauren stared down at the phone as it rang, feeling her nerve slipping away with each passing moment.

She hadn't spoken to Allie in years, and when she had, it had been nothing more than the obligatory small talk that usually sufficed for former childhood friends.

She was a respected police officer living a day's drive away. She had no reason to pick up the call. Besides, it was getting late. Cody's work wasn't the sort to be done during normal daylight hours. Allie was probably relaxing in front of a Netflix show by now with a glass of wine. It was a total waste of–

"Parker," came a voice from the phone.

"Oh, Allie, hi, sorry to call so late," Lauren stammered. "It's me."

She flinched as soon as the words came out. How would Allie know who 'me' was?

"It's Lauren. From El Paso," she added quickly.

She heard voices on the other end of the line. "One second," Allie said.

"Yeah, I gotta take this. Five minutes. I'll be there." the woman continued, her voice muffled.

Great. She wasn't at home on her couch. She was at work.

"Sorry, Lauren," Allie said. "How are you? Is everything okay?"

"If it's a bad time, please, I won't bother you," Lauren said. "I should have texted first–"

"I told you to call me if you needed to, any time, day or night," Allie said firmly. "I meant it."

Lauren paused.

She remembered that conversation well.

It was the last time she'd seen Allie in person, about three years prior. She and Lauren's mutual high school friend had been killed in a drive-by shooting, and Allie had traveled from El Paso for the funeral.

Cody had hung around in the cemetery to sell weed to several of their old classmates, and Allie had caught on.

Instead of getting him in trouble, however, she'd pulled Lauren aside and told her that if she was ever ready to leave him and to leave the Iron Prophets, Allie would be there. No questions asked.

"Lauren? Are you still there?" Her voice crackled a little over the speaker, and Lauren made her way closer to the living room window. The reception in their building was spotty, and at least here she'd be able to see if Cody's car showed up. He'd probably be gone for hours, but it wasn't like he'd call her to let her know he was coming home early if he changed his plans.

"Yeah, sorry, I'm here," Lauren said, hating how pathetic she sounded. Maybe this whole thing had been a mistake.

"So what's up?" Allie asked.

The background noise was gone, and Lauren felt a fresh pang of guilt for taking her away from her work. Still, now that she'd made the call, she couldn't exactly pretend to be asking her how her summer had been. She may as well tell the truth.

"I–I think I've really gotten in over my head," she said, pressing her eyes shut as she forced the words out. "Cody has a big deal coming up, he wants me to help, and I don't think he's going to take no for an answer."

The line was silent for a moment, and Lauren could picture Allie taking out a pad and a pen, ready to jot down every detail.

She was taking a risk, and she knew it. Her old friend had promised to help her, but at the end of the day, she was still a cop.

But what better choice did she have?

She tightened her fist until her fingernails dug into her palms. If there was any hope of getting out of the mess she'd found herself in, Allie Parker was it.

"A drug deal, I'm guessing. Who are the players?"

"The Iron Prophets and the cartel," Lauren replied meekly.

"Do you know which cartel?"

She didn't. Her gang only worked with one.

"Just that they operate out of Juárez."

"Good. Any names you can give me? Any big players you know about?"

"I just know that Cody works with a guy called El Pez. I've met him. He scares me."

She heard Allie suck in a breath.

"Okay, Lauren. He's gotten himself quite a reputation, even down here in San Antonio. Not the kind of man you want to be doing business with."

"I know," she said, biting back frustration as she peered out between the curtains again. She saw two teenage boys she recognized strolling through the parking lot below, but there was no sign of approaching headlights.

"What exactly does Cody want you to do?" Allie asked, her voice taking on a kinder, less business-like tone. Perhaps she'd set her pencil aside.

"He told me he needs me to run the drugs from point A to point B once they arrive in Texas. He didn't tell me any other details. I just know that none of the guys he'd trust with that amount of product have a clean record, and I do."

"He wants you to smuggle the drugs within the State of Texas," she echoed.

"Yes."

Allie swore. "I'll be straight with you. That puts us in a bad position."

She said nothing, gripping the phone more tightly between her fingers. A bad idea. She knew it. She should have dealt with her problems herself.

"It's one thing if you confess to me that you're planning to break the law under the jurisdiction of Mexican law enforcement, but if you're here in Texas, it complicates things. I can still try and get you a deal, and I do have connections with the DEA, but I can't promise much–"

"Forget it. Just forget I called," Lauren said, surprised at the force in her voice. Allie was right. Her record was clean, but her history certainly wasn't. The last thing she needed was the DEA at her doorstep.

"Wait, wait, wait," Allie said quickly. "Don't hang up."

"I don't want to go to jail. I just want out. I'm sorry. I'll figure out another way."

"Lauren."

She drew in a breath, releasing it slowly as she pressed her forehead against the window. Suddenly, all she wanted to do was to go to bed.

"What?"

"The police aren't the only ones who can help you," Allie said. "I work closely with a local company called Forge

Brothers Security. They're actively involved in fighting back against various players in the drug trafficking game, as well as other criminal groups."

Lauren considered this. If they weren't actual cops, it was likely they had more leeway when it came to working with people like her.

"Anyway, if you'll let me, I can call them tonight and set up a meeting. I'm sure they'll agree to send an operative down to El Paso if it means getting some inside dirt on the Iron Prophets and on El Pez."

"How will I meet with anybody without Cody knowing?"

Allie let out a sigh. "These guys know what they're doing. When I have more details, I'll put you in touch with your contact there and you can figure out a plan. Start brainstorming how you can get out of your house for a few hours sometime in the next couple of days."

"Okay."

Lauren stood there, staring out at the darkness of the parking lot. Cody was out there somewhere. What he was doing or who he was with was a mystery to her. Usually, his attitude upset her, especially when she suspected other women were involved, but at the moment she felt only numbness.

Before Allie could say more, there was a rustling sound on the other end of the phone line, followed by a group of loud voices.

"Okay, I have to get back," her old friend said quickly. "But if you need anything before I get in touch, call me back, okay? Lauren?"

"Okay. I can do that," she said at last. "Thanks, Allie."

"We'll get you out of this," she said gently. "Just hold on."

REILLY

"In two miles, your destination will be on your right."

Reilly listened to the cheerful voice of the GPS coming through the speakers of his rental car as he drove down the narrow street, trying to take in his surroundings.

It never ceased to surprise him just how different El Paso's climate was from San Antonio's, despite the fact that it had only taken him a couple of hours to fly here.

At the outskirts of town, with smaller buildings and fewer wide highways, the difference was even more apparent. The desert sand and the mountains seemed to be pressing in toward the area, as though reluctant to cede any space to human habitation.

Reilly pulled up to a red light, tapping at the steering wheel impatiently as he waited for a handful of cars to pass through the intersection. He hadn't seen any tumbleweeds, but their presence wouldn't have surprised him.

When he'd spoken to his contact, Lauren Ortega, the night before, she'd warned him that the address of the park where they were meeting was isolated.

He couldn't blame her for her caution.

He'd spent most of his time at the airport and on his flight digging deeper into the Iron Prophets gang, and what he found made it clear why she wanted to get out. They didn't play around, and he was hopeful that he'd be able to talk to her today without incident.

His phone rang where he'd left it in his cup holder, making the plastic rattle.

"This is Reilly," he said, fumbling for the speakerphone button.

"Are you there yet?"

Their police liaison, Allie Parker, rarely bothered to say a proper hello. Especially not when they were working a case.

"Just about," he said, pulling up to yet another red light. This time, not a single car crossed in front of him.

On the sidewalk to his left, he saw two young men in baggy pants walking side by side, jostling one another and laughing. There were no retail businesses here that he could see, not even a corner store. Only run-down bungalows and a few buildings that might have been offices in better times.

"Lauren just texted me. Says she's wearing all black and sitting on a bench near the south edge of the park. She doesn't have a lot of time to talk, and you're late."

"Okay," he said, trying not to let his frustration show as he glanced at the clock on the dashboard. He'd just traveled halfway across the state, and already the informant was complaining when he was less than ten minutes late? "I'll be right there. Two minutes. Sorry."

Allie hung up, and at last he saw the small park. It consisted of a patch of dry, brown grass with a couple of small play structures in the middle, surrounded by a rusting chain-link fence.

He pulled his car over along the side of the road, hoping that the decent rental sedan wouldn't draw too much attention. It was nicer than any of the other vehicles he'd seen in the area.

As he strode into the park, he pulled at the edge of his basic gray t-shirt, making sure the butt of his pistol was well concealed. People were used to seeing guns in Texas, but he didn't want anyone to get the idea that he was anything other than a local out for a stroll on a fine late-summer day.

There were several children playing, their mothers watching from benches or pushing them on swings, and a group of teenage girls giggling over by a graffiti-covered water fountain.

And then he spotted his contact.

He forced his hands into his pockets and kept walking in

her direction, despite wanting to pause for a moment and take in what he saw.

Despite the very short black skirt, mesh top, and heavy makeup that she wore, the woman was gorgeous. Her wavy dark hair fell around tanned shoulders, and her brown eyes looked almost amber in the sunshine.

Reilly forced himself to smile at her as he approached, in case he accidentally let his jaw fall open. What she looked like didn't matter. Even though she wanted help from FBS to get out of the Iron Prophets, for the moment, she was both a drug smuggler and petty criminal. Even if he had time to think about dating, which he most certainly didn't, he was a security operative. Women like this did not belong on his radar. At all.

No matter how much her unexpected beauty had instantly rendered him stupid.

"Hey, I'm Reilly Forge," he said, sitting down on the bench beside her. A piece of faded green paint flicked off and fluttered to the ground, and he stared at it for a moment, trying to get himself together.

From everything Allie had told him, this was going to be a serious operation, and he needed to keep his head in the game.

"Lauren Ortega," the girl said, her voice harder than he'd expected, almost defensive.

"Sorry I'm late," he said, meeting her eyes and giving what he hoped was a charming smile. "It was a bit of a trip, and then they gave me the wrong set of keys to my rental car at the airport."

She nodded. "It's fine, I'm just–yeah, it's fine."

Reilly glanced around, half-expecting to see the woman's boyfriend or another gang member lurking along the fence, but there was no one.

"I take it you don't have a lot of time to yourself," he said carefully.

She gave him a small smile. It was enough to make her entire face light up. "Cody likes to know where I'm at. Not that he gives me the same courtesy."

"Boyfriend?"

He already knew exactly who Cody Deller was, of course. Allie had given him a rundown on Lauren's background. But it didn't hurt to hear a little about her situation from her own perspective.

"He's just a little protective," she said, a hint of defensiveness returning to her tone. "But in the circles we're in, it's kind of dangerous not to be. Rival gangs, cops–no offense–"

"I'm not a cop, so none taken," Reilly said, grinning.

"–there's a lot of people out there who could be a threat to me. So, yeah, I don't have long to talk. I had to take three buses to get here, and I don't know exactly when he'll get home. I want to be there when he does."

Reilly nodded.

"Thank you for coming. It took guts, and I appreciate it, Lauren," he said gently.

He saw a blush rising beneath her tawny cheeks.

"Right," she said. "Anyway, like I told Allie, my boyfriend is trying to get me to take part in a big drug deal with the cartel, and he's not going to just let me walk away if I refuse. It's the last straw, and I need help." She looked troubled as she spoke, as though admitting to any sort of weakness was painful.

Perhaps it was, considering that she'd been a member of the Iron Prophets since middle school.

"Allie briefed me," Reilly said, nodding. By the sounds of it, they didn't have time to get into as much detail as he'd like. "I already talked to my brother, Gabe–he's technically the leader of our company–and he's agreed to put the resources of Forge Brothers Security behind you.

"If you can help us to thwart the deal, we can make sure you get a fresh start. We'll set you up somewhere, offer

17

protection, the whole thing. It'll take a few more days to get the logistics fully organized, but the basic plan is worked out. We will need to move forward right away, though, if we want to be set up by the time the deal goes down."

As he spoke, she fiddled with her cell phone in her lap, kicking her legs back and forth under the bench. All at once, she looked more like a nervous teenager than a full-grown woman in her mid twenties.

"I have to think about it," she said at last. "I need more time."

"Look, I know that it couldn't have been an easy decision to reach out to Allie–"

Before he could say more, she cut him off, her eyes flashing with annoyance.

"I've known her since we were kids, but no, it wasn't. And she never said anything about me having to make a decision about putting my life on the line without a second to breathe."

"You're putting your life on the line either way," he countered. "Otherwise, why would you be trying to get out?"

She crossed her arms over her chest as she glared at him.

"You have a point. But I need to know that I can trust you not to flip on me to the pigs as soon as this is over," she said.

Even though he wasn't a police officer himself, he couldn't help but to flinch at her casual use of such degrading slang.

"You've already confessed to Allie that you've worked as a mule before," he pointed out. "If the goal was to string you up, I could have done it already. So could she. You're a small player, Lauren. We're interested in going after El Pez and some of the higher-ups in the Iron Prophets. If we can help you in the meantime, that's even better."

He watched the muscles in her jaw relaxing slightly as she searched his face.

"Well aren't you Mr. Debate Club president," she said at last, defeated.

Reilly couldn't help but to smile. "I almost flunked out of high school, actually, but I'll take the compliment."

She scoffed, but he could see the hint of a smile on her full pink lips.

"Okay. I'll work with you," she said. "But I need to know what's going on. I've had enough of being pushed around like a pawn."

He nodded. "You will, as soon as I figure it out on my end. Let's get you home. I can drop you off–"

"No. I'm fine."

"You said you took three buses to get here," he said gently. "We'll be careful. It's not like anyone here is going to recognize me."

"No!" she snapped, shaking her head forcefully. "It's not worth it. My boyfriend always has friends watching the place. People will notice if I show up with some strange guy with a decent car."

Reilly clenched a fist against his side. "Your boyfriend sounds like a real winner."

As he watched Lauren's face fall, he immediately wished that he could rewind a few seconds and keep his big mouth shut.

"Look, you're right," Lauren said. "Cody isn't perfect. If he was, I wouldn't be here talking to you right now. I wouldn't be trying to walk away. But you're still not getting it."

He opened his mouth to say that he was sorry, but she pressed on.

"I know for a good guy like you, all you see when you look at the Iron Prophets are a bunch of worthless gang-bangers. But you're wrong. We're real people. We look out for one another. We're a family, and for a lot of us, the gang is the only family we have.

"And even though I'm getting out and choosing something different for my life, I'm not going to hate the people who made me into the person I am. Not even Cody. If you want me to help you bring down the top dogs in the gang, as well as El Pez and the cartel, I need you to at least respect that."

She glanced down at her lap as she finished, tucking a strand of dark hair behind her ear.

"I understand," he said finally.

He didn't deny that he often saw gang members as exactly how she described. It was difficult not to, when so much of his life consisted of helping victims of crime to get their lives back.

But he did understand her dedication to the people she saw as her family, even as she was forced to betray them in order to free herself.

His family situation was unconventional, too, and though he highly doubted that his adoptive family would ever behave like the members of the Iron Prophets did, he could imagine the difficulty of the position she was in. No matter what his uncle or his cousins did, he'd never be able to stop caring about them.

"I really do need to start heading back," she said, breaking the silence that had fallen between them.

Across the park, several of the women had begun rounding up their children for what Reilly could only assume was afternoon nap time.

His flight back to San Antonio wasn't until later that evening, but it was time for him to get out of Lauren's way.

"Take some cash for the bus, at least," he said, reaching into his wallet and handing her several bills too many. To his relief, she took them without complaint.

"Thanks, Reilly," she said, giving him the softest hint of a smile.

For a moment, her eyes lingered on his, and he found himself saying a silent prayer that she would overcome the odds, and find the path that God had planned for her.

He cleared his throat, breaking the spell.

"You're welcome," he said. "I'll be in touch as soon as I have the next part of the plan locked in, but if you need me before then, don't hesitate to call. Safe travels."

She slid off of the bench and he watched as she walked away, giving the park a final once-over before he got up himself.

It was time to get to work.

CHAPTER
THREE

LAUREN

Lauren hated the bus.

She'd chosen a seat near the driver, far from the teenagers goofing around in the back, but it was still too loud. All she wanted was a few moments to reflect, but the previous two legs of her trip had been just as annoying, and when she got home, she'd have Cody to deal with.

It was exhausting.

With a sigh of resignation, she pulled her headphones out of her pocket and stuck them into her ears, opening a music streaming app. As the sound of wailing guitars filled her head, she found it easier to think.

She couldn't decide whether or not she'd made a terrible mistake. Guilt pierced at her heart as she considered what she'd told Reilly Forge.

All of it was true.

Ever since her *abuelita* moved to a nursing home, the Iron Prophets were the only family she had. But how could she say so, while in the same breath agreeing to betray them?

She leaned her head against the cool glass of the bus

window. The sound of a heavy drum riff pounded against her skull, and she watched as several shabby storefronts whooshed by. They were getting closer to her neighborhood, and she still had no idea what to do.

Even if she wanted to call the whole thing off, would Allie let her walk away?

Would Reilly?

He was a whole other complication. She'd been expecting some middle-aged guy with a mustache and a beer belly. Instead she'd found herself face to face with a tall, dark, and handsome stranger.

Worse still, he seemed to look at her the same way she'd caught herself looking at him.

The last thing she needed was some goody-two-shoes security guard distracting her from the task at hand.

After a few more songs, she'd arrived at her stop, and when she pulled the bell cord, she was relieved to see that no one else was getting off of the bus with her.

She couldn't risk getting off at her apartment complex–she didn't want Cody to think she'd gone any further away than walking distance–but even in the late afternoon, this wasn't a great neighborhood. Multiple gangs crossed this area, and she had no interest in spending much time outside of the Iron Prophets' turf.

As she walked the several blocks toward home, she ran possible excuses over and over in her mind.

By the time she'd headed up the smelly old elevator and reached her front door, she figured she knew what to say, even if he was home earlier than she expected.

Drawing a breath, she jabbed her keys into the lock and turned the door handle.

Before she registered what was happening, she felt Cody's thick arms gripping her shoulders and dragging her into the dingy room.

"Cody–"

Her protest was cut off as he slammed the door behind her, loud enough that every neighbor on their floor would be able to hear.

Not that it mattered.

How gang members handled their wives and girlfriends was their business.

"You think you can do anything, huh?" he shouted in her face. His words were slurred.

She hadn't expected him home until later that night, but by the looks of it, he'd had plenty of time to sit around stewing over a case of beer.

"Please let go of me," she said, trying to stop her voice from shaking as he shoved her toward their bedroom. "We can talk."

"Talk? You think I wanna talk to a streetwalker like you?"

"What are you–"

"You think you gonna run around on me? Do you?"

Before she could respond, he'd thrown her down on the bed. She hit her wrist off of her nightstand, but she bit back her cry. Better her wrist than her head.

"Cody, I would never do that," she said, hardening her voice so that she wouldn't let any sobs escape. She'd learned from experience that showing weakness always seemed to make him even more angry, and he was already more ticked off than usual.

"One of our girls saw you at the park with some military-looking guy."

"What? Who?"

"Camila. You callin' her a liar?"

Lauren brought a hand to her forehead, trying to think of everyone she'd seen at the park today. She certainly hadn't seen her friend Camila hanging around, but it hardly mattered now.

If Camila had seen her, Lauren could hardly blame her for

snitching. She was probably just trying to avoid a beating of her own.

"Who was he, Lauren?" Cody demanded, pacing back and forth in their bedroom like a caged tiger. She didn't dare get up from the bed.

"I remember some guy asked me for a smoke," she lied, forcing herself to meet Cody's glare. "But that was it. I barely spoke to him for two seconds. Camila clearly misunderstood the situation."

"What were you doing all the way in that park?"

"What was Camila doing there?" she countered, unable to hide the flash of anger rising in her voice. "A client, right? Some guy who works close by who wanted his girl delivered for his lunch break. Well, that's why I was there. One of the guys I sell dope to asked if I could deliver today, so I did."

She cringed as the lie came out of her mouth. Her grandmother had always hated lying, no matter the reason, but what choice did she have?

"You're a liar," he said, stopping short and walking back over to the bed. She pushed herself back against the pillows as he towered over her, his eyes dark with fury. He clenched a fist, and she flinched, sure that he was about to hit her, but at the last second, he pulled away again.

"Get out of my house," he said instead, his words low and dangerous. "You can find somewhere else to sleep tonight, and give some serious thought to just how seriously you plan on taking this job. If you ain't gonna be loyal to me, you had better wise up and be loyal to the family."

She stared at him. The threat was clear.

No one was going to take her side. Thanks to Cody's rank in the gang, everyone would make sure that she was punished.

She walked past Cody's simmering gaze and pushed her way out into the hallway, glad that her phone was still in her pocket.

As she made her way to a nearby fast food place, she tried to figure out an alternative to what she was about to do, but nothing came to mind.

Her friends were loyal to the Iron Prophets first. They couldn't help her even if they wanted to.

But Reilly had given her his number.

At the moment, he was the best option she had.

REILLY

Reilly's phone rang just as he retrieved his shoes from the plastic security bin.

Great timing.

"Gabe, I just got through security," he said by way of greeting, grabbing the last of his belongings and striding across the filthy airport floor in his socks. "Can this wait until–"

"It's Lauren."

He paused, staring at nothing as the crowd surged past him in search of their gates. She was the last person he'd expected to hear from, but the tone of her voice made his gut clench with worry. Had one of her boyfriend's goons followed Lauren, or otherwise seen them together? Had Cody himself?

"I thought you'd be on a plane right now," she said, stammering, the confident tone she'd displayed earlier completely erased from her voice. "Sorry. I should have just waited. Just forget it."

"No, wait, don't hang up," Reilly said a little too loudly. A couple of women with big Texas hairstyles stared at him, whispering to one another as they pulled their wheeled carry-on bags across the tile. "I told you to call if you needed anything. What's going on?"

For a second she didn't speak, and he could hear voices in the background. If she wasn't alone, she could be in even more trouble than he thought. If her gang thought she was snitching, the consequences could be deadly.

"Someone saw us together," she said at last. "But she assumed I was cheating with you, not planning to thwart a drug deal."

His relief was short-lived.

"But the news made it to Cody before I got home, and he was furious. He threw me out tonight and—and I have nowhere to go."

"Where are you right now?" he asked, already making his way toward the exit. He'd have to find his checked luggage later.

"I'm just at a fast food place. Burger Wizard," Lauren said, rattling off the address.

"Were you followed? Does anyone else know you're there?"

"I don't think so," she said. "But I can't be sure. I'm within our usual territory."

He swore under his breath. It was going to be dark out soon, and he didn't want her wandering the streets at night or holing up somewhere dangerous, but being close to the other Iron Prophets was a big risk. He could only pray that she'd somehow escape notice until he got there.

"Stay put," he ordered as he strode through the sliding doors, leaving behind the comfortable air conditioning of the airport for stifling desert heat. "I'm coming to get you, and if anyone has a problem with that, they'll wish they hadn't."

He surprised himself by the anger in his voice. Usually, he was good at staying calm and professional, but the thought of anyone hurting Lauren—especially that scumbag boyfriend of hers—filled him with rage.

"You have to be careful," she pleaded. "If someone sees you a second time, it'll prove to Cody I'm a liar."

He considered this. As much as he wanted to come in

guns blazing, she was right. This operation was going to require him to be a little more delicate.

"Okay, fair enough," he said, releasing a slow breath. "I'll think of something. Just hold on."

LAUREN

Lauren lowered her head as the teenage employee passed by her table, sweeping old french fries into a pile as she went. The girl looked about as happy to be here as she was, but at least she hadn't said anything about the fact that Lauren had been sipping a glass of water for the last half hour rather than actually buying anything.

Still, she was nervous.

She'd already seen at least five people that she knew, and the only reason they hadn't seen her was because they'd all stayed near the front counter and hadn't noticed her lurking in a back corner booth. Getting in without being seen had been a miracle in itself, but getting out would be even more risky.

Just then, her phone began vibrating in the front pocket of her skirt, making her jump.

She yanked it free as the buzzing went silent. It was a text.

"Go to the counter and ask for a large decaf coffee with three sugars, then head for the bathroom. Someone will meet you there with a change of clothes. Just a precaution. After you put them on, keep your head down and come out front. I'll be there."

She glanced down at the screen and read the words a second time.

Suddenly, the whole situation seemed completely absurd.

Why was she trusting Reilly, anyway? She barely knew the man. Maybe it wasn't too late to walk back to the apartment and beg Cody for forgiveness.

But before she could consider whether or not to bail, she saw two women come in that made her breath catch in her chest.

They were clearly Prophets. Both were dressed like she was, in tight dark clothes with lots of makeup, but they were at least a decade older. Their cheeks were sunken and hollow, as though they hadn't eaten a proper meal in weeks, but their eyes were what had caught her attention.

Both of the women looked lost, miserable, and broken.

There was no spark left. As they strode toward the counter, they reminded Lauren of zombies.

She had come face to face with the reality of her future.

If she didn't show up for the drug deal, she'd be lucky to live long enough to tell about it.

But even if she was able to walk away from Cody and his side of the business, she'd end up just like them—addicted and selling her body on the street.

And after that… she didn't even want to think about it.

Her own happiness and fulfillment was irrelevant. The good of the gang was what mattered. Perhaps these two women had figured that out, but by now, it was probably too late for them.

The chance at a normal life had passed them by.

Lauren got to her feet and walked toward a trash can, her eyes roving between the two doors of the restaurant as she went.

The two women had gotten their sodas and headed back out toward the parking lot. The coast was clear.

She forced herself to put one foot in front of the other as she made her way toward the counter to place the coffee order Reilly had commanded.

She had nothing left to lose.

CHAPTER
FOUR

REILLY

"All right, Lauren, let's go," Reilly said to himself as he watched a group of women meandering across the parking lot, talking and laughing as they went.

The sun had set, taking the edge off of the searing August heat. Better yet, the darkness provided some level of anonymity as he sat in his rented black minivan. It was in better shape than most of the cars parked nearby, but that couldn't be helped. So far, no one had given him so much as a second glance, and he figured he fit in well enough.

He peered through the window, scanning the expanse of asphalt once again for any sign of trouble.

At last, he saw Lauren coming out of the front entrance, dressed in a full Burger Wizard uniform with the visor pulled low over her face. She was almost unrecognizable.

Perfect.

Grace Hinton, the office manager for Forge Brothers Security, had pulled off one of her miracles, this time from across the state. He wasn't sure exactly how, but she'd managed to convince one of the employees at the restaurant to switch clothing with Lauren, providing a perfect last minute disguise while he whisked her away from the Iron Prophets' turf.

As his informant reached for the passenger door handle, he noticed at once that she seemed to have nothing with her, save for the cracked cell phone she grasped in her other hand.

"We have to go. I know those girls," she said, pulling the door shut behind her as she settled into her seat. "And I saw some other guys just before you messaged me. Cody might be on his way here. I don't know. I want to get out of here."

"Put on your seatbelt," he ordered.

She complied without protest, but he noticed that her hands were shaking as she clipped the buckle into place. With a final glance through her window, she slid down in her seat.

Reilly tightened his grip on the steering wheel, picking up on her nervous energy in spite of himself.

He hoped she was paranoid for nothing, but there was nothing he could do to change the situation now. Either way, he had to get her out of here.

"Can we go?" she snapped.

He raised an eyebrow as he shifted the car into gear and stepped on the gas.

When they had left the parking lot, Lauren laid back against her seat, closing her eyes.

"Sorry."

"It's okay," Reilly replied, keeping his eyes on the darkened streets ahead.

Everything about her body language indicated hardness and anger, but he had lived long enough to sense that there was more beneath the surface.

Fear.

Helplessness.

But could there be something more?

Was it possible that he'd been able to offer Lauren some much-needed hope?

No matter how prickly she was, he couldn't help but to

want to keep her safe. He caught himself glancing in her direction as they pulled up to a stoplight, searching her pretty face for answers to questions that he wouldn't dare ask.

He couldn't get attached. He wouldn't.

She was an informant that could help him and his brothers to thwart the Iron Prophets and to deal a major blow to the cartel.

Nothing more.

LAUREN

"Where are we going, exactly?"

Lauren opened her eyes and sat up straighter in her seat as they continued to make their way through the streets of El Paso.

She knew this area. It was much nicer than the part of town where her gang took up residence, but it wasn't wealthy enough that her presence would draw attention.

Glancing down at her clothes, she felt a smile rising to her lips. She had forgotten that she wasn't wearing her own clothes. The Burger Wizard uniform made her look about a decade younger. She could easily pass for an average suburban teen with a summer job.

"To find you a place to sleep," Reilly said, turning the wheel of the van smoothly and driving into the parking lot of a large Walmart. "But before that, I thought you might like something more comfortable to wear to bed, and some food."

She nodded as he slid into a space near the far end of the lot, where the light from the streetlights barely touched.

"Wait for me here. If anything happens, you call me, okay? Stay out of sight, just in case."

She nodded again.

"Sure."

Satisfied, he got out of the van and she watched as he

strode confidently toward the front doors. The store was still busy, and for a moment, she realized just how much she wanted to follow him in. Wanted to walk beside him, like two normal people–maybe even a couple–shopping for a few groceries.

She fiddled with the dials on the dashboard and turned down the air conditioning, frustrated with herself. She shouldn't even be trusting this stranger, let alone indulging in ridiculous fantasies where a guy like that would ever have anything to do with a woman like her.

A half hour or so later, after making a second stop at a hole-in-the-wall Chinese place to grab takeout, they finally reached their destination.

Lauren gaped as Reilly pulled up to the nicest hotel she'd ever seen, leaving her to wait in the pull-through while he checked in.

She didn't bother to crouch in her seat this time. No one she knew in the Iron Prophets would be able to afford to actually stay in a place like this, not in a million years. And any gang members who might be here would be more worried about not getting caught selling drugs or hooking than keeping an eye out for her.

She sighed, shaking her head as she watched Reilly talking to the well-dressed man at the front desk. In case she hadn't felt inferior enough, she now could safely assume that her benefactor was not only smart and handsome, but rich, too.

By the time they had reached the elevator, Lauren had barely spoken two words to him. She was too busy taking in the plush carpets, the rich warm lighting, and the general aura of grandeur.

She'd grown up in a cockroach-infested bachelor apartment with her grandmother. For the first several years of her life, she'd been given the twin bed, until *abuelita*'s back pain started. After that, she'd taken up residence on the ancient pull-out couch, falling asleep to the sound of telenovelas on the tiny TV that sat in the corner of their single room.

She'd never met her father, so far as she knew, and her mother was an addict who spent more time in jail than out of it. As much as she appreciated all that her *abuelita* had done for her, it hadn't been an easy way to grow up. Even though she was half white, when she began kindergarten, she barely spoke a word of English. Neither the latino kids nor the white kids had accepted her, and she was bullied relentlessly.

When she started high school and met Cody, everything changed. Once she became a member of the Iron Prophets, she found not only protection, but acceptance, and eventually a little bit of money.

Still, even though her and Cody's apartment was a step up from the abject poverty she'd been raised in, this hotel made it look like a complete dump.

"You're in 6016 tonight," Reilly said as he stepped out of the elevator, handing her a keycard.

For a moment, she stared at his outstretched palm.

She was really going to stay here tonight. Safe, cozy, and surrounded by luxury. She felt like her old life was already a thousand miles away.

"Thanks," she said at last, taking the slender gold card and scanning the doors for her room number as they walked.

"This one's me," he said as they came to a stop in front of 6018. "Why don't you go next door and shower, or whatever you want to do to settle in, and then we can eat together?"

He sounded so earnest that she couldn't help but to smile. Until that moment, she'd been excited to go to bed nice and early, but spending a little more time talking to him first couldn't hurt.

She allowed herself to linger in the shower for a few minutes longer than necessary, savoring the strong water pressure and the hot steam until her stomach began to growl with hunger.

When she reached into the Walmart bag and found the pajamas that Reilly had picked out for her, she couldn't help but to chuckle. She was used to the tastes of the men around her, and the modest cotton two-piece set and matching robe were the total opposite of what Cody would have gone with.

Once she'd dressed, she took a moment to peer through the peephole of her door, and then stuck her head out into the hall. It was empty.

"Knock, knock," she announced as she rapped on Reilly's door, running a hand through her hair for a final time. She'd scrubbed off her makeup, and she couldn't help but to feel naked without it. She'd leave her usual messy bun for when she returned to her room. At least with her hair down, she could hide her face a little.

Not that she cared what he thought of her looks.

Not much, anyway.

"I'm about to die of hunger," he said by way of greeting, ushering her into his room and handing her a cardboard takeout box. "And when's the last time you ate?"

"I can't remember," she said honestly, popping the top of the box open as she sat down on the thickly carpeted floor. Despite the amount of time that had passed, the food was still fairly hot, and it smelled amazing. "Breakfast, I think."

Reilly threw a packet of disposable chopsticks in her direction. "Sheesh. I ate at the airport. I feel bad for complaining."

She glanced over at him as she started to tuck into her food. By the grin on his face as he started munching on a chicken ball, he hardly looked contrite.

As they ate, she glanced around the room. It was identical to her own, with two huge beds covered in pristine white sheets and a view of the city lights through the window. She wondered if she could sneak into his bathroom before he left and borrow a spare bottle of the expensive-smelling shampoo she'd used during her shower.

All of a sudden, a memory flashed in her mind, and she stopped chewing mid-bite.

"You okay?" Reilly asked, sticking his chopsticks into a half-eaten container of fried rice.

"Fine," she said quickly, swallowing the chicken she'd been eating in a thick gulp.

"You don't look fine," he said.

Lauren set her own chopsticks aside and leaned against the end of the bed.

He had an infuriating way of being able to read everything written on her face, no matter how much she tried to hide what she was really thinking.

She'd always assumed that she had a good poker face, but maybe that wasn't the truth.

Maybe it was simply that no one else in her life cared enough to really look.

"You can talk to me, you know," he added.

She felt her heart pick up speed as he shifted his body closer to her own, giving her a playful jab in the ribs with his elbow.

"You've been through a lot today. It might be good for you to rant a little."

She paused, considering her words carefully.

Perhaps she'd go with honesty for once.

"It's hard to talk to you," she admitted.

Reilly placed his fingers against his chest in mock offense. "I'll have you know that I'm very understanding. I have a reputation in the Forge family for giving good advice and keeping the peace. It's a tough job, but someone's gotta do it."

Unlike her, he made no attempt to hide the teasing look on his face. He was an open book.

"You're so...normal," she said. "It's hard for me to believe you'll understand where I'm coming from, that's all."

"Try me."

Her breath hitched as he rested his fingertips against her forearm. The touch lasted barely a second, but it had been enough to knock her firmly off balance.

"It was just something I remembered from when I was a kid. Like, a really little kid. It doesn't matter."

"Sure it does," Reilly countered. "Much of who we are is shaped by things that happen early in life. Even before we can talk."

"I take it you're also the Forge family shrink?" she joked, pulling her knees toward her chest.

"I'm serious. I want to know."

His eyes caught hers, and for some reason, she suspected that there was more he wasn't saying. Did he want to know about her past because it would help them work together better, or did he—for whatever insane reason—actually want to get to know her?

"Well," she said at last. "I visit hotels quite a lot. Everything from decent ones where higher-level gang members stay to motels where addicts live full-time. The Iron Prophets don't mind making deliveries of our products. For the right price, at least."

"That sounds dangerous, especially for a woman working alone," Reilly chimed in.

She nodded. There was no point in denying it.

Sometimes, she carried a gun, but it didn't do much to calm her nerves when she had to knock on a door in some crappy motel complex. Even though she mostly dealt to those that the gang had vetted, drugs made people unpredictable. She could never be sure what would happen.

"Anyway," she continued, "I just realized that I've actually been to this hotel before. I must have been five or six."

Reilly said nothing, but the cheerful look on his face was gone, replaced with concern.

She set her jaw.

She didn't need his pity, but it was too late to tell him off for prying now.

"My mom had a rich client, some executive from Dallas or Houston or something. He stayed in this hotel when he came to El Paso. I remember one night she brought me here while she worked, and I stayed in the bathroom. I spent an hour playing with the shower cap and the empty soap boxes. And then she took me home."

"Your mother brought you with her to a prostitution job?" he asked, his dark eyes narrowed.

Lauren felt heat rising to her cheeks. She should never have shared her shameful history. Of course he wasn't going to understand.

"My mom had nobody to help her, and I'm guessing she was busy. I'm sorry that my childhood wasn't as perfect as yours."

As soon as she saw the look on Reilly's face, she regretted her words.

He was right.

Her mother had messed up, big time, but admitting it somehow made her feel even worse.

"My parents died in a car accident when I was five," he said after a long pause.

Lauren felt like she'd been slapped.

"I didn't–I shouldn't have–I'm sorry."

Reilly turned toward her, his brown eyes catching hers. She could smell the leathery scent of his cologne.

And she'd just opened her big mouth and insulted him.

"I didn't tell you that to make you feel–"

Before he could get his full sentence out, his phone started to ring, vibrating where it sat on the carpet next to the box of spring rolls they'd devoured. The name 'Gabe' was lit up on the screen.

Reilly picked it up and hit the speakerphone button.

"Hey, Gabe. Lauren can hear you, too. What's going on?"

"Nothing good," the man on the other end said.

He paused.

Reilly caught her eye and shook his head, letting out a sigh.

"Don't tell me that, bro," he said.

"Don't shoot the messenger," Gabe countered, his voice free of humor. "Apparently, there's been a little mix-up with your deal. It's just been bumped up to 48 hours from now, and if you want this plan of yours to work, I suggest you figure it out fast."

REILLY

"The deal has been pushed up?" Lauren was echoing, her voice choked with panic. "Cody's deal? My deal?"

Reilly turned to face her.

He let his eyes linger on hers for a second longer than necessary before he spoke.

"Where'd you get the intel?" he asked Gabe.

Lauren looked puzzled, and he wished he could explain to her that though she was their primary informant on the case, FBS had plenty of contacts and connections of their own, even here in El Paso.

"Straight from one of our trusted men in Juárez," Gabe said. "Apparently, there's already been some tension brewing with the manufacturer and our gang boys here, and the cartel is thinking about pulling out. They told Thomas Crown himself that either the deal goes through in the next two days, or they're done."

Lauren's eyes lit up with recognition, and Reilly gave her a quick nod.

Crown had a somewhat lower rank within the Iron Prophets that El Pez enjoyed in his cartel, but still, he was a big player. He wondered how much Lauren knew about him.

Before he could say more, he heard Lauren's phone beginning to beep. He waited for it to go silent, but instead, the tone just kept chiming over and over.

"Let me call you back," Reilly said. "I have some stuff to figure out on our end. Keep on it back at the office. It'll work out, somehow."

"48 hours, bro."

Gabe hung up.

"Are you okay?" Reilly asked, glancing down at the pile of notifications that were covering most of Lauren's screen. He didn't want to read over her shoulder, but he couldn't help but to notice that every single message came from her boyfriend.

"He's looking for me," she said. "He just heard about the job being moved, by the sounds of it, and he isn't happy. He told me I have to get home."

Reilly wanted to grab the phone and tell the jerk that if he hadn't tossed Lauren out of their apartment, she wouldn't be here with him now, but he restrained himself.

"Have you said anything back?"

Lauren shook her head, glancing up at him for a moment before continuing to scroll through the messages.

"It's just the usual stuff. He's sorry, he shouldn't have gotten so rough, blah blah blah. I'm so tired of hearing it."

Reilly leaned his head back against the foot of the bed, trying in vain to gather his swirling thoughts.

All he wanted to do was to keep Lauren by his side, where he'd know for sure that she was safe. But the operation had to come first.

"What should I tell him?" Lauren asked, her voice barely above a whisper.

More than once that day, he'd managed to tick her off, but at that moment, the look in her eyes was unmistakable. She trusted him, at least for now. And he wished he had something better to say to her.

"If we want to get you away from the gang long term, you need to go back," he said after a moment. "You need him to think you've forgiven him and that everything is okay. And then you need to go through with the deal."

CHAPTER
FIVE

LAUREN

L auren looked past Reilly, listening as a cascade of sirens sounded somewhere outside of the open hotel room window.

For a minute, she'd let herself feel safe.

She'd let herself look forward to sleeping in a comfortable bed, wrapped up in expensive sheets, imagining a life that would never belong to her.

She'd even managed to forget the way she'd covered her ears as she hid in the bathroom all of those years ago, not wanting to think about what was going on outside.

Reilly's words tore everything away in an instant, leaving only numbness behind.

She'd finally found the courage to seek help, and now the reality of what that would look like was sinking in. Allie had been right from the start. It was complicated. She was never going to be able to just run away.

But that didn't mean she'd expected to have to go crawling back to Cody so soon after he'd put his hands on her.

"Are you okay?" Reilly asked, reaching out and resting a hand on her shoulder.

She shrugged away from him as though his touch had burned her.

"He was really angry before he kicked me out."

She looked down at the carpet, but she could hear the fury in Reilly's voice as he spoke.

"I know. Trust me, I hate to let you get within fifty feet of that degenerate piece of trash."

She flinched at the comment. If Cody was a degenerate piece of trash, she wasn't much better.

"FBS has already started putting together a plan for the day of the drug deal, ever since I talked to Allie," he continued. "You'll be monitored constantly, and backup won't be far away. We were hoping to have more time to set up, but–"

"And until then, what?" she snapped, raising her head until his face was inches from her own. "I go to sleep next to my boyfriend with a wire under my clothes, just hoping he doesn't find out?"

Reilly said nothing for a moment, but he held her gaze, and she could see the tangle of emotions behind his fierce brown eyes.

"Our surveillance tech is a lot better than what you see on TV," he said calmly. "You don't have to worry about it. I promise. I'm going to be nearby, as close as I can get, until the big deal. And during it, of course. Cody isn't going to do anything. Not if you can keep your head down for a couple of days."

Lauren felt her throat growing tight, but she swallowed the sob that was threatening to escape. She didn't cry. And if she was going to start now, she wasn't about to do it in front of Reilly Forge.

She might have seen empathy in his eyes, but at the end of the day, he was simply doing his job. She might be able to follow his lead, but fully trusting him was another thing entirely.

"I just don't want to be used," she said, unable to stop the catch in her voice. "I'm going to be taking most of the risk. I believe that FBS is going to try to keep me safe, but there's a cartel and a gang on the other side. Do you understand what men like this are capable of?"

Reilly's expression darkened.

"I don't have time to talk about it now, but believe me, I do. I spend a lot of time around evil men, Lauren."

She opened her mouth to speak, but he continued.

"I want to help you to get out of this pit you're buried in, but it's give and take. Getting you out is going to cost tens of thousands of dollars and put my own brothers and our employees at risk, too."

She felt a pang of guilt. She hadn't considered that, but it made sense. Starting over wasn't going to be free, and she wouldn't be the only one with a target on her back in the end.

"I'm sorry," she said.

"I don't want you to apologize," he said firmly. "I just want you to understand. Think of everyone out there, dying of overdoses. Think of the suffering that fentanyl has wrought in your community and so many others.

"God has put you in a position where you can help not only FBS and law enforcement, but all of Texas. All of America. Heck, even the citizens of Mexico will benefit if we can chop a couple of heads off of the endless cartel hydras. You can do something really important."

She couldn't help but to feel a surge of attraction as he spoke, his passion for justice clear in every word his deep voice pronounced. Reilly was honorable. It wasn't a trait she saw much of, and it drew her to him whether she wanted to be pulled in or not.

Still, she had to keep her head.

Virtuous words were refreshing to hear, but they meant little on the street.

"If this fails, I'll have nothing left," she said after a moment.

"Right now, you have a membership in a violent gang and a boyfriend who puts his hands on you," Reilly pointed out.

His words stung, but she couldn't argue.

"I know. But you need to understand that they're the closest thing I have to a real family."

As soon as the words slipped out, she wished that she could take them back, but Reilly didn't look offended.

"I didn't get a chance to tell you this before, but I have a real family, too," he said, moving a few inches closer. His arm brushed hers for a split second, and she felt goosebumps prickling at her skin.

She seriously needed to get it together.

"My uncle Gabriel and my aunt Mary adopted me. She died of cancer, but before that, she was like a mother to me. They always treated me like I was their own, and I never really felt like an orphan. I'm really blessed."

"They sound like amazing people," Lauren ventured.

"They are. And then I had–have–their sons. All five of my cousins treat me as an honorary Forge brother."

He smiled, no doubt lost in hundreds of happy memories.

"What about you?" he asked. "You must have somebody. Somebody other than the members of the Prophets."

Lauren glanced up at him. "I do, actually. My grandmother raised me after my mom ended up in prison, and she's still alive. I shouldn't have discounted her. She's my family, both by blood and by love, but it's different now. She has dementia and lives in a nursing facility. She isn't lucid that often, but I always try to see her when she is."

She paused as realization hit.

"Though I guess that's going to be a lot more complicated after this job."

Reilly shook his head and extended a hand toward hers. Without thinking about what she was doing, she placed her small hand within his larger one, accepting the warmth of his touch.

"I'm making it official. Making sure your grandmother is safe is part of the deal. We'll find a way to make it happen so that you can still visit her. She stepped up and took care of you, and dementia or not, she deserves to have you in her life."

Lauren bit her lip, certain that the tears really would fall this time.

"I told you I was going to protect you," Reilly said gently, letting his thumb trace gentle circles against her skin. "I don't just want you to get out of the Iron Prophets. I want you to find a better life."

His touch sent shivers coursing through her, and he began to lean in even closer.

"Reilly," she said as she drew her hand away, knowing that she had no choice but to break the spell, "why are you doing this? Why are you so willing to help me?"

For a moment, she felt the air growing hazy between them once again as she considered whether it would be completely stupid to reach out to take his hand back.

Fortunately, before she could move, he was pulling away, running his fingers through his short hair.

"Because you're a beautiful daughter of God, and you deserve a second chance," he said, giving her a soft smile. "And that's worth whatever risk I have to take."

She couldn't decide whether to be thankful, or to argue.

Before she could speak, however, he had already gotten to his feet and begun picking up the remains of their takeout dinner, shoving empty boxes and discarded chopsticks into the trash can that sat under the hotel room's desk.

"You should text your boyfriend and tell him that you'll be home first thing in the morning," he said, barely looking up from his task as he consolidated leftover rice, shrimp, and steamed broccoli into a single container. "You need some rest, and he needs time to cool off."

She took out her phone and typed out a short message, hitting send by the time Reilly had finished. She got to her feet and yawned, stretching her arms over her head. The tiredness seemed to have hit her all at once.

"Thank you," she said when he turned to face her again. "For everything."

"You're welcome," he said simply, reaching for the duffle bag that sat at the foot of his bed. "I'll be sleeping right here. Don't check your phone until morning. Let Cody be mad if he's going to be mad."

"Okay," she agreed, making a show of picking up the device and turning it off. He was right. She was willing to grovel and say whatever she had to to make him believe she'd forgiven him, but not yet. She was going to enjoy a few more hours of peace first.

"If you need anything–"

"Wake you up," Lauren finished. "I will. Good night, Reilly."

"Good night."

A few minutes later she was in her own bed, pulling the clean comforter up beneath her chin. The door was locked, the chain was in place, and she hadn't felt so safe for as long as she could remember.

The fact that a handsome private security operative was sleeping next door didn't hurt, either.

She let out a sigh as she stared up at the ceiling.

Reilly had brought up God, and now she found herself with the crazy idea that maybe she should pray.

It had been a while. Years, even. She definitely hadn't willingly said a prayer since before her *abuelita* got sick.

She closed her eyes and turned onto her side, clicking off the lamp at the side of her bed.

What she really needed was a good night's sleep.

Maybe Reilly really did think that she deserved a second chance.

But she doubted that God would want to take her back.

Not after who she'd become, and everything she'd done.

CHAPTER
SIX

REILLY

The sun was rising in pink and gold by the time Reilly had finished his shower, ordered room service, and settled in front of his laptop. He'd planned to stay in bed a little longer, but sleep hadn't come easily. He'd woken up in the night more than once, worrying in the dark until finally his exhaustion took over.

He jiggled his finger on the trackpad, trying to pay attention to the brief that Gabe had sent over to him several hours before.

He couldn't focus.

He had almost kissed her last night, and he was pretty sure that she had wanted to let him.

Worse still, despite the fact that getting close to her was incredibly dangerous, part of him still wished that he had.

He opened up his email program and began composing a reply to Gabe. The plan he had spent all night coming up with looked solid enough, but Reilly knew it would take a little more finessing before it was completely ready.

Until then, he would try to share as little detail as possible.

There was no point in stressing Lauren out over things that could still change.

There was a knock at the door, and he closed the lid of the laptop and headed over to look out of the peephole. By the looks of it, she hadn't been able to sleep that well, either.

They shared good mornings, and a few minutes later, room service arrived with pancakes, eggs, and bacon.

"Thanks for breakfast," she said as she sat down next to him on the floor again. "It looks great."

"When this is all over, hopefully we can eat together at a real table sometime," he joked, immediately wanting to kick himself when he saw her expression.

"I mean, if I'm able to help out with your relocation," he added quickly. "They're still figuring out options back at the office. It's not an area I work in very much."

"Right," Lauren said, spearing a piece of bacon with her fork and shoving it into her mouth.

An awkward silence fell, and he pretended to be deeply focused on his glass of orange juice.

For the moment, she was an informant, and busting up the drug deal had to be his top priority. But after it ended, why was he so certain that they had to stay apart?

He'd meant what he'd said the night before. Jesus loved her, and she deserved a second chance.

Maybe that included a second chance at being with a man who would actually treat her with respect.

"So," he said, breaking the silence between bites of pancake, "are you feeling ready for your last two days in the Iron Prophets?"

She gave him a slight smile.

"I guess that'll depend on how many raging texts Cody sent me last night. I haven't looked yet. Do you mind?"

His eyes widened as she held out her phone toward him.

She was offering him at least a little bit of her trust—and better still, she was allowing him to offer her some emotional protection. As far as Reilly was concerned, it was progress.

His mood soured as soon as he turned on the device.

There were at least twenty new messages since last night, moving schizophrenically between pleading apologies and fits of frustration until they stopped around four in the morning.

Most importantly, though, there was nothing that indicated to Reilly that violence would be imminent if Lauren returned.

"So?" she asked, setting her fork and knife down on her plate in front of her.

"The bad news is that he's still a total jerk," he said, shaking his head. "The good news is that he's almost certainly still asleep, so we have a little more time to get you home."

To his surprise, Lauren didn't look scared.

If anything, she looked happy.

"Wait, you are just pretending to go back to him, right?" he said, trying to give her a playful wink that he knew wouldn't quite conceal the seriousness of his question.

"Sorry, it's not that, I just–I can't believe that if we pull this off, I won't have to go back. I won't have to keep living this empty, hollow life any more. I actually get a fresh start. A future. I hadn't really imagined myself as having much of a future in a very long time."

Reilly felt an aching in his heart. Lauren had no doubt made many of her own terrible decisions, but the more he spent time with her, the clearer it had become that what she needed most of all was compassion. Her life had been difficult in a way that his hadn't. What would he have chosen, if he'd faced the same circumstances?

"Your fresh start has already begun," he pointed out. "You've chosen a better path forward, and God is going to be with you every step of the way."

She paused for a moment, glancing out the window. As the morning sun fell upon her cheek, Reilly's breath caught in his chest. Sitting here with him, without makeup, her hair up in a messy bun, she looked just like an angel.

"God doesn't seem very interested in me," she said at last. "But then again, it's not like I've really gone looking for Him, either."

Reilly knew that feeling. Even though he'd been a Christian all his life, that didn't mean he'd never endured dry seasons where he questioned his faith.

He decided not to press the issue. Most of the people Lauren associated with would probably lash out at the very mention of the Lord's name.

One step at a time.

"You ready to play pretend?" he said instead, gesturing toward the suitcase that stood near the desk.

Lauren nodded. "Cody will be looking for me soon. Let's do this."

LAUREN

The bus smelled like feet.

Lauren wrinkled her nose, glancing out the window as she tried to stop herself from fiddling with the hidden cameras that were sewn into her clothing.

None of the other people on the bus had noticed anything, and logically, she knew that no one else would, including Cody. Most of the devices looked like no more than a tiny button or a fashionably-placed rivet. But she couldn't help but to be nervous.

She pulled down the tight black t-shirt she wore, trying to cover the strip of tanned stomach that kept escaping as the bus bumped over the streets of El Paso. Forge Brothers Security's office manager, Grace, had sent over a couple of different surveillance-enhanced outfits, and Lauren was surprised by just how closely they resembled clothes that she already owned.

Though she vastly preferred them to the borrowed Burger Wizard uniform, she found herself feeling suddenly self-conscious about the tight pants and somewhat sexy tops.

Maybe Reilly's good little church boy thing was rubbing off on her, or maybe she just wanted to explore a new style for her new life, but for the moment, she knew it was necessary that Cody see her looking exactly as she usually did.

She'd been expecting a bulletproof vest or something, but Reilly had told her that they couldn't risk it or even an earpiece. She'd be too close to her boyfriend to hide much, especially at night.

Still, before she'd left the hotel, he'd assured her that he could see everything she saw and hear everything she heard, and that he'd be just down the street if anything went wrong.

His cousin Cameron had been trying to fly in from San Antonio since the wee hours of the morning, but there'd been some delays. Last she heard, he was still struggling to find a flight, but she trusted he'd get there as soon as he could for backup.

She heard the ding of the bell overhead signaling that someone wanted to get off, and realized that they had already passed the terminal station without her noticing.

She watched as a couple of older women got off, dragging their patterned grocery trolleys behind them. The bus was quiet this time of morning, and she was thankful that she'd gotten a few minutes to think without the usual crowd of teenagers loudly goofing off at the back.

Once they were moving again, it took only another ten minutes before the stop she wanted appeared through the windshield. She tugged at the yellow wire, listening to the cheerful beep as the driver began to slow, and tried to quell the anxiety that was bubbling in her gut.

She stepped off the bus and onto the sidewalk, which was

strewn with several takeout cups and cigarette butts. So far, she was alone, but she wouldn't be for much longer.

So much could go wrong, and she had no idea what she would do if it did.

Reilly had assured her that everything would be okay, and when he was sitting there beside her, she believed him.

Now, in the harsh light of day, things looked very different.

She kept her head down as she made her way through the familiar streets of her neighborhood, not wanting to draw any unwanted attention to herself. Just being seen returning to Cody in the early morning hours would be enough to set off gossip that they simply didn't need. Not to mention that there was always a risk that the last of the drunks and junkies might not have gone to bed yet.

Wherever FBS planned to help her get set up, she hoped that it would be a lot safer than the Iron Prophets' territory. She'd lived in ghetto neighborhoods all her life, and she'd come to accept the inherent threat of danger as normal, but she knew that it wasn't.

She doubted that Reilly Forge and his employees had to worry about being held up for crack money on their way to work, but it had happened to her more than once.

Finally, she reached the familiar cluster of brown apartment buildings and headed toward the back door of her block before realizing that she didn't have her keys with her.

Great.

She backtracked toward the front doors, passing two carefully spray-painted murals and several messy tags depicting male appendages.

"Yo, Ortega," shouted a voice from across the parking lot, making her jump.

As she turned to see who it was, she relaxed. It was only Camila's kid brother waving at her from the bus stop. By the looks of it, he was stuck attending summer school once again instead of sleeping away the last days of his vacation.

She waved back at him before turning back to the building and locating her apartment on the ancient buzzer box.

She hesitated. Cody was probably sleeping, and wouldn't be thrilled to be woken up. On the other hand, she couldn't exactly stand around out here waiting for everyone else to wake up.

She jabbed at the button with a chewed thumbnail and waited.

After just two rings, she heard Cody's voice blaring over the blown speaker.

"Lauren? Where were you?"

"I–"

"Get inside. Now."

She heard the line click, and a second later, the front door of the building unlocked.

Apparently, the being-nice-and-begging-for-her-to-come-back part was already over.

With a final glance behind her, wondering where Reilly was hiding out, she stepped into the building and made for the elevators.

She already had her ticket out of here. She just had to hold on until tomorrow night.

CHAPTER
SEVEN

REILLY

"Okay, see you in five," Reilly said, hanging up the phone call with Cameron and breathing a sigh of relief.

He glanced out the window, watching as the sun began to dip below the top of the apartment building, bathing the parking lot in shadows. He saw three young girls in what looked to be party dresses stumbling toward the bus stop, but aside from that, nothing seemed to be going on save for a few teenage boys smoking on a nearby fire escape.

It had been one of the most boring days of his life, and for that, he was thankful.

He had spent the entire day in the van Grace had procured for surveillance, watching Lauren's camera feeds for any sign of trouble, but none had ever come.

Still, he hadn't been able to relax, let alone take the nap he so desperately needed after his terrible sleep the night before.

He could have asked one of his employees to keep an eye on the cameras remotely, back in San Antonio, but he didn't.

He wanted to know for himself, every moment, that Lauren was okay.

He'd watched her arrive that morning, and immediately he'd wanted to rush in and pull her out of the operation, but he knew it would be foolish. Instead, he listened throughout the day as Cody Deller berated her, called her names, and generally acted like the world's biggest tool.

But he hadn't done anything physically threatening, and if he stepped in and ruined the operation without just cause, Gabe would be furious. He might even refuse to use FBS resources to relocate and protect Lauren.

That wasn't a risk that Reilly was willing to take.

Fortunately, Cody had left for most of the day, and he'd watched as Lauren cooked lunch for herself and cleaned the apartment from top to bottom. It was a total disaster, with clothes piled everywhere and what appeared to be an entire shelf of DVDs dumped on the floor.

He wondered if it had been that way for a while, or if Lauren's boyfriend had flown into a rage when she'd left and left a nice mess for her to clean up. Either way, he wasn't going to bring it up and risk embarrassing her. Soon enough, she'd be out of this place and living somewhere decent. He'd make sure of that.

At last, he heard the screech of brakes and turned to look out the passenger side window just as his cousin, Cameron, emerged from the bus.

He couldn't help but to chuckle as he watched him crossing the parking lot of the apartment complex, carrying a coffee in each hand and a duffle bag slung over his shoulders.

Reilly was just wearing jeans and a plain t-shirt. Cameron now sported frosted tips in his hair, sagging black pants, and a long sleeve shirt that looked like it had come from a skate shop.

"Please tell me this is a disguise and not a new look," he

said as Cameron climbed into the passenger seat of the van. "Please."

"Ha-ha," Cameron said, pretending to withhold the large takeout coffee cup against his chest. "Grace has way too much fun with jobs like this. I told her I'd be staying in the van if humanly possible, but she insisted that I take extra precautions."

"She didn't try it with me," Reilly said, gesturing toward his own, normal outfit.

"It's harder to threaten you from across the state," he said with mock gravity. "Trust me, if she thought she could play Reilly's Extreme Makeover, she would have."

Reilly reached over and took the coffee, taking a grateful sip while Cameron shoved his duffle bag into the back. He'd been careful not to drink too much over the last several hours, considering the fact that a van lacked a bathroom.

"So what's been happening? Any action?" Cam asked, flicking through the video feeds on the console laptop one by one.

Reilly passed him an earpiece.

"There hasn't been for several hours. But look who just got home," he said, frowning at the screen.

The two men watched as Cody strode into the apartment's living room, tossing his hooded sweatshirt, pack of cigarettes, and sneakers onto the floor that Lauren had just finished vacuuming.

The small act of disrespect was enough to set Reilly's teeth on edge, and his annoyance only grew as Cody's voice came through his earpiece.

"I just saw Ryan and Dez. I think Ry is gonna bail on helping out."

"Oh," he heard Lauren say, her voice clear on the mic. "Is it a big problem?"

"What do you think, genius?" Cody snapped. "Do you

think I want to lose a guy the day before the biggest hustle of my life? Huh?"

Lauren said nothing.

At the moment, Reilly was glad that Cameron was here. The thought of storming in there and throwing a punch or two was more than tempting.

As though reading his mind, Cameron glanced over at Reilly and shook his head, and the two of them watched as she picked up her boyfriend's discarded items from the floor and began putting them away.

"I'm sorry, baby girl," Cody said after a few tense moments had passed. "I'm just on edge. I thought I'd have more time to sort these morons out. Everything is rushed."

"Look, it's okay," Lauren said, giving him a sweet smile. Over the camera, Reilly couldn't see if it reached her eyes or not. "You can handle this. Thomas Crown trusts you for a reason. This is your chance to prove yourself."

Reilly watched as he collapsed back onto the couch, rubbing at his temples. "Funny you brought him up."

"Who? Crown?" Lauren asked, settling in beside him.

Her acting was good, Reilly had to admit. If he didn't know better, he wouldn't have suspected that she was anything but loyal.

Cody nodded.

"He's going to be there tomorrow. At the job."

"Really? Why?"

Reilly would have asked the same question. It sounded like whatever was going on with the cartel, the Iron Prophets, and their fentanyl manufacturer was a big deal.

"I don't know," Cody said, sounding exasperated. "It's nothing for you to worry about, anyway. You just do what you're told to do and it'll be fine, whether he's there or not. No one's there to stare at your rear end, not that I'd blame them if they did. It's all about the money, babe."

Cameron caught his eye and raised an eyebrow, and Reilly forced himself to unclench his tightened fists.

Cody's piggish commentary aside, this was good news for FBS. By the sounds of it, they might have a chance to nab not only El Pez, but Thomas Crown, as well.

For several minutes, neither Cody nor Lauren said anything else, and Reilly felt himself relaxing a little. He might even risk a trip to the bushes behind one of the apartment buildings for a slightly more dignified bathroom break.

Before he could say anything, however, Cameron broke the silence.

"You know, I really hope we can help Lauren. It's gotta take guts for her to be willing to help us. And her boyfriend seems like a real piece of work. Wild to me that a guy like that can get a girl, and yet you and I are still single."

His cousin gave him a pointed look.

"Yeah," Reilly said, the words seeming to get stuck in his throat. "Right."

Cam knew him well. Too well. And he didn't like where this conversation was going.

"Gabe seems to think you're feeling a little bit protective of our informant here," he said, prodding at Reilly's ribs with his elbow and nearly knocking over his coffee. "Like maybe she's, I don't know, getting under your skin."

"She's not."

Cameron looked over at him and raised an eyebrow, waiting.

"Fine. I've enjoyed being around her, that's all. I want to help her."

"And she's really pretty."

"And, yes, she's really pretty," Reilly admitted, rolling his eyes. "But it doesn't matter. She's an informant, and the op comes first. I can't afford distractions."

Cameron didn't look convinced, but he settled into his

seat and looked at the laptop screen again, watching as the couple moved around their living room in silence.

Reilly did the same, but his thoughts were elsewhere.

Cameron's gut instinct was right. He was falling for her, whether he'd meant to or not.

After the operation was over, Lauren was fair game. If she was interested in seeing where things went.

But even if she was, was he really going to be able to give a damaged woman like her what she needed?

LAUREN

Lauren spent the next fifteen minutes trying to busy herself with cleaning the apartment, but after spending most of the day on the project, there wasn't much left to do. Still, dusting the TV stand for the fifth time was preferable to sitting there wallowing in her worries about tomorrow's job.

With less than 24 hours to go, Cody hadn't bothered to explain to her exactly what she'd be doing or where she'd be taking the fentanyl. And Reilly's plan was still somewhat up in the air.

She could only hope that everything would come together in time, and that he and FBS would keep her safe like he promised. There was nothing else she could do.

Cody's phone rang, and she listened as it vibrated against the freshly-wiped coffee table.

"Yo, B-Dawg," he said by way of greeting.

Lauren looked over with mild interest until she saw her boyfriend's face fall.

"I'll be there. See you in ten."

She watched as he stormed into their room, putting on a dark hooded sweatshirt and stuffing his gun into the back of his jeans.

"What's going on?" she asked, following him to the doorway. "Did something happen?"

"It's Camila," he said, shaking his head. His voice was shaking, and Lauren felt her heart beginning to race.

She waited as he pulled on his sneakers and tied the laces, desperately wanting to ask for more information, but knowing that if she pushed, he'd probably tell her to mind her own business and leave without another word.

"She was working on Parkleaf tonight. Got beaten by a john. She's in the hospital."

Lauren drew a hand to her mouth, horrified.

"I'm going to deal with the scumbag responsible. You'd better be here when I get back."

Without another word, he left the apartment, slamming the door behind him.

Lauren collapsed onto the couch. The room suddenly felt as though it was spinning.

Even though Camila had told Cody about seeing her with Reilly, she was still her friend, and the thought of her being harmed made Lauren feel sick.

Every john in the area knew that messing with one of the Iron Prophet hookers was a death sentence. Usually, it was enough to keep them safe on the street as they worked–well, as safe as one could be while selling her body for sex–but apparently Camila had run into a particularly suicidal pervert.

Tears pricked her eyes as she picked up her phone, watching as a flood of text messages from friends came in, informing her about what had just happened.

She wanted to go to the hospital and look for her, but of course she didn't dare.

One of the messages caught her eye.

"I'll meet you on the fire escape. Delete this."

She read it a couple of times. It was Reilly.

After deleting the text as instructed, she slid open the sliding door and stepped onto the narrow fire escape, narrowly avoiding sticking her bare foot into the empty coffee can that she and Cody used to hold their cigarette butts.

Without a word, Reilly pulled her against his body in a tight embrace, and despite her best efforts to hold her pain inside, she felt hot tears spilling onto her cheeks.

She was scared for Camila, but even more than that, she realized that she was angry, too, and not just at the john.

She hated that Reilly and the guys at his company knew her business, and were now getting a front-row seat to the shameful reality of life in the Iron Prophets.

"It's risky for you to be here," she said at last, swiping the sleeve of her shirt over her eyes as she pulled away. "Someone might see you."

"My cousin Cameron agrees. He finally arrived, and now he's helping me on camera duty," Reilly said, pointing toward a large white utility van across the parking lot. "But I thought you needed a friend."

Lauren said nothing as she stared down at her feet. Despite her humiliation and despite the risk to the operation, she couldn't help but to feel touched by his gesture.

"Not to mention a reminder that it'll be okay. God sees you, and he sees Camila. Cameron's in the car praying for her right now, and I'll be doing the same. I'm so sorry this happened."

He reached out and took her hand, doing nothing but look at her for several impossibly long seconds.

Even in the yellow glow of the cheap outdoor light, he was unbelievably handsome.

And kind-hearted.

And dedicated to his faith.

All she wanted to do was to move closer to him, cameras or no cameras, but she knew it would be foolish.

How could she even think about letting someone as good as he was into the wreck that was her life?

She forced herself to step back, letting her hand fall away from his own and turning toward the sliding door.

"Thanks, Reilly," she said, tugging at the handle until the glass panel slid free.

"Anytime."

With one last smile that she hoped conveyed all of the words she didn't have the courage to say, she retreated back into the apartment.

CHAPTER
EIGHT

REILLY

Reilly's entire body ached.

He pressed his eyes shut tight as he tried to shift his weight in the driver's seat of the vehicle. He sat there quietly for a few more minutes, half-hoping that he might be able to catch another hour of sleep, but it didn't take long for him to give up.

The morning light flooded the cab of the van, illuminating Cameron's own sleep-deprived face. He had bags under his eyes, and his newly-frosted hair was sticking up in all directions.

He was already looking at the laptop screen, though Lauren's cameras showed nothing but, presumably, the inside of the covers on her bed. Cody had never returned to the apartment, and he wondered what sort of fate had met the john who had beat on the girl they called Camila. Eventually, he'd have to tell law enforcement what they'd learned, but for the moment, it was low on the priority list.

"Morning. You look terrible," he said, stretching out his arms over his head and letting out a jaw-splitting yawn.

"You too, bro," Cameron replied cheerfully, reaching into a pocket on his door and passing Reilly a protein bar. Reilly took it, tearing into the foil package with his teeth and taking a bite of the chalky beige substance within. All he wanted was a hot cup of coffee, but this would have to do for now.

"Maybe Gabe should have taken this job himself," Cameron said. "He loves getting three hours of sleep."

Reilly laughed. It was true. Gabe got up before five every morning, usually to go spend an hour at their office's gym before starting work early. Even after sleeping in a surveillance van, he'd probably be downright perky by this time of morning.

"Speaking of Gabe, is he going to tell the law about the bust yet?" he asked.

Cameron shook his head. "I asked him to. So did Ben. But he says he doesn't want too many cooks in the kitchen. Our best contact in the DEA is currently on medical leave, and we don't have a lot of close contact with El Paso PD."

"I can see his logic there," Reilly said, nodding. "They could also try and kick us off the op. And if they did, they'd almost certainly lose Lauren, too."

"That's true," Cameron said, letting out a sigh as he glanced out the window. The parking lot was still free of human activity for the moment, though a lot of cars had shown up to park throughout the night. "I guess I'm just kind of salty that we're taking all the risk, and in the end we'll be handing over El Pez and Crown to the cops so they can take all the credit."

"I know," Reilly said. "But I'll tie them each up with a satin bow if it means getting those scumbags off the street. We have a higher mission than our own glory, right?"

Cam nodded. "Fair enough. But it's a big mission for three people. And Ben's not even here in person."

"Four," Reilly corrected. "We have Lauren, too. If Gabe handed this to the law, they'd have nothing but brute force to work with. I really do think that we have a better shot at this than they would."

"Speaking of Lauren, Gabe nailed down some of the particulars," Cameron said carefully. "He ran through the plan with me while you were passed out."

Reilly tried to relax as Cameron laid out the basics of the plan, but the more his cousin spoke, the more anxious he became.

"I'm gonna call Gabe and tell him he needs to think of a plan B. This is way too dangerous," he said at last, gripping the steering wheel in front of him with white-knuckled fists. "If anything goes wrong, she's dead."

"Despite your boneheaded choice to go all Romeo on her balcony last night, you need to keep your personal feelings out of it," Cam said sharply. "Lauren knows the risks. If she wants her freedom, this is what needs to be done."

Before he could argue, he heard a rustling sound coming through his earpiece, followed by the slamming of Lauren's apartment door.

Cameron angled the laptop toward him, and they both watched in silence as Lauren walked into the living room, just in time for Cody to stride into the apartment with a huge bouquet of flowers in his arms.

"Those for Camila?" Lauren asked.

Cody looked pained. "I did drop off some for her this morning, but no, these are for you."

Reilly wished that he could see Lauren's expression as she took the bouquet from his arms and headed toward the kitchen for something to put them in.

Cody leaned against the counter as she turned the sink on and filled an old mason jar with water.

"I'm sorry, princess," he said, looking down at his feet. "I've been a real jerk the last couple of days, and last night–"

"What, seeing what it would be like if you lost control of your anger knocked some sense into you?" Lauren snapped.

Reilly glanced over at Cam, who continued to stare intently at the small screen. If Lauren freaked out on her boyfriend now, it could end badly. It was crucial that she maintain her cover.

"I'd never hurt you like that," Cody said, his voice gentle. "I promise you that, okay? I shouldn't have pushed you. You're right. I messed up, and I'm so sorry. Will you forgive me?"

Reilly was thankful that Lauren wasn't wearing an earpiece. The answer he would have advised her to give would almost certainly ruin the operation.

Cody spoke again before Lauren could offer a response.

"Oh, and Camila is awake today, and looking a lot better already. She wants to see you, and I told her I'd bring you by tomorrow, just as soon as we get this thing tonight over with. Does that sound like a plan, babe?"

Lauren used a pair of scissors to chop off the bottom of the flowers' stems before lowering them carefully into the jar.

"Yes to visiting Camila," she said. "As for the forgiving you part, I don't really know what to believe any more."

Reilly tensed as he watched Cody move toward her in a couple of quick strides, determination on his face.

Instead of doing anything threatening, he reached up a hand, he leaned in for a kiss.

"Oh, just what I need before seven AM," Cam said, making a fake gagging sound, but Reilly barely heard him.

Lauren seemed to be pressing herself against Cody's chest, not hesitating or pulling back, even as the kiss continued for several impossibly long seconds.

He knew he should look away, but he couldn't seem to tear his eyes away from the laptop screen.

She was clearly comfortable with him. According to the intel Allie had given him, they'd been together for years. The fact that Lauren wanted out of the Iron Prophets wouldn't automatically sever that connection, no matter how awful Cody clearly was.

Finally, the kiss ended, and Reilly pretended to be very interested in rooting around in his overnight bag for his toothbrush as his cheeks burned.

"You good?" Cam asked when he looked up again, raising an eyebrow.

"Why wouldn't I be?"

His cousin shook his head. "Look, man. At the end of the day, we can only trust Lauren so much. And there's a reason the Bible cautions us against being unequally yoked."

"Yes, dad," Reilly said, giving Cam an exaggerated eye roll.

Only problem was, he was right.

Abused and traumatized women usually went back to the men who'd hurt them in the end. That was reality. And for Lauren, whose only family support came from a gang, this was even more likely.

This informant wasn't the only one risking her life in this operation.

He and Cameron were, too.

And if she flipped on them, the consequences would be deadly.

LAUREN

Lauren looked up from the grilled cheese sandwiches she was preparing as the doorbell sounded.

"That'll be Dez and Lily," Cody announced from his spot in front of the television, making no move to get up.

Lauren set aside the bread and cheese and took a couple of deep breaths before heading over to answer the door.

Despite the sunflowers that now brightened up the dull kitchen, Cody's romantic mood clearly didn't extend to actually getting off the couch. He'd spent the entire morning smoking and watching Seinfeld reruns.

Having finished most of the housework the day before, she'd had little to occupy herself. She had tried to do some reading, but it was impossible to focus. Tonight's operation loomed over her head like a dark cloud.

"Hey, guys," she said, slipping the lock-chain loose and pulling the door open. "Where are the little ones today?"

Lily scoffed, tossing her blonde hair extensions over one shoulder. "Staying with family again, thanks to CPS."

"Maybe if your mom would stop poking around our business, they'd leave us alone for a while," her boyfriend, Dez, grumbled.

Lauren gave what she hoped came across as a sympathetic smile. She didn't like Cody's best friend nor his girlfriend very much, and though she felt bad that they had once again failed to parent their kids properly, she couldn't help but to be relieved that their twin boys weren't currently running around tearing their apartment apart.

"Come take a seat, guys," Cody said, patting the scratched leather couch. "Lauren's making us some lunch."

"Give me another ten minutes," she said, giving them a tight smile as she disappeared into the kitchen once again.

As she buttered bread and tore open packaged cheese slices, she tried to listen to the conversation taking place in the living room, but she didn't understand much of it. It sounded like the two men were talking about a job from a few months back rather than what they'd actually be doing tonight.

She pressed the spatula down hard against the grilled cheese that sat in the frying pan, frustration rising. The job was hours away, and she still had no idea what she was doing.

All she wanted to do was talk to Reilly. Hopefully, by now, he and the rest of FBS had been able to pull together a plan–

though it would be a lot easier for them if she could get Cody on camera explaining exactly how things would be going down.

Just as she carried the paper plates of grilled cheese into the living room, Cody's phone rang.

She set the plates down in front of her guests, half-listening to his conversation, until she heard Cody beginning to raise his voice.

"Maybe show some respect, lady," he was saying. "I'm good for it. Yeah, today. Okay. I'll be there, just—"

He pulled the phone away from his ear and looked down at the screen, calling the woman on the other end a word that Lauren had never particularly liked.

"Everything okay?" Dez asked through a mouthful of grilled cheese.

"My car got impounded, can you believe that?"

"It's not in your parking space?" Lily chimed in, giving them all the courtesy of swallowing her food before she spoke.

"No, it is. That's what I don't get. They took it anyway. Now they want cash."

He was already on his feet, stuffing his wallet into the front pocket of his jeans and making for the door.

"You can't seriously be thinking of paying up?"

"We need the car for tonight, Dez," Cody snapped. "It's all worked out already. I don't have time to find another one. Finish up your lunch, and then head back to your place to finish getting ready. I'll meet you there as soon as I can."

"Do you really want the cartel knowing what you—what we—drive?" Lauren cut in, her stomach twisting with unease. Cody may have been a gangbanger, but he wasn't stupid. And using your own vehicle for a drug deal was about as dumb as cooking meth in your own house.

"See? She learns quick," Cody said, grinning at Dez as though she wasn't even in the room. "Normally you'd be

71

right, princess, but it's a little different this time. The cartel wanted to know up front what vehicles to expect in case any unwanted visitors show up, and it was easier to tell them ahead of time to look for my car."

"Right," she said, though she remained unconvinced. Even though she'd soon be well out of reach of the cartel, she didn't want Cody getting hurt over something so foolish.

"Don't worry. We'll have enough money after tonight that I'll be buying us a new car in cash. You and the drugs will be in our old car just until you hit the drop off, and the pick-up guy will torch it then."

Lauren forced herself to take a breath before saying anything.

Finally, some information that Reilly could use.

"Will you be with me?"

Cody shook his head. "You'll be alone, but like I said, let me do the worrying. You'll be fine."

With a final wave to Dez and Lily, he headed out into the hall.

Lauren chewed her own sandwich without really tasting it, listening politely as Lily told her all about her latest shoplifting exploits at the outlet mall, oblivious to the fact that two private security operatives were hearing every word.

At last, the couple finished eating, and after a couple of awkward goodbyes, Lauren was finally alone.

She waited on the couch, staring out the window until she saw their pickup truck driving away. She released a sigh of relief as she got to her feet.

If she was going to find the strength to go through with this, she had to talk to Reilly. And by the sounds of it, this might be the last chance she had.

CHAPTER
NINE

"What's she doing?" Cameron asked, looking intently down at the laptop.

Reilly clenched his jaw, leaning over the screen and watching as Lauren stepped out of her apartment and onto the fire escape where he'd met her the night before.

It was a risky move. It was daytime now, and using the same meeting place twice was always a risk. He half expected her to message him and let him know that she was just stepping out for some air, but his phone remained stubbornly silent.

"I should text her, I guess," he said. "See what she wants."

Cameron gestured toward the screen. "She left her phone inside."

The two men watched as several people passed beneath Lauren's fire escape. She was high enough up that it was unlikely anyone would hear her, but someone on the ground would have a decent view if they backed up a little.

Question was, how closely was Cody really watching,

even after Lauren's friend had told him about their little meeting in the park?

"Do you want me to go?" Cam asked. "Prince Charming knows what you look like."

Reilly hesitated. Logically, he had a point.

Although they were cousins and bore some resemblance to one another, Cameron had blue eyes instead of his own brown ones. Furthermore, he lacked Reilly's half-native-American coloring and features.

On the other hand, if Lauren was freaking out about the night ahead, she'd be looking for reassurance from someone she trusted.

At last, he shook his head. "I'll go, but I need you watching my back."

"Always, bro," Cam said, grabbing a small plastic object out of his front pocket. "Just make sure you get this to Lauren."

"Will do."

He stuffed the tiny earpiece into his own jeans and headed across the parking lot. As soon as the coast was clear, he darted up the stairs as quickly as he could until he reached Lauren's floor.

"I can't stay more than a couple of minutes," he said at once. "Your boyfriend will be back soon."

Just the mention of Cody made him feel sick inside. He couldn't help but to imagine him kissing Lauren. Worse, he kept imagining the way that she'd kissed him right back.

"How do you know?" she asked, stepping backward until she was partly concealed by the building's shadow. He followed.

"The impound lot thing was a ruse, thanks to Grace back at the office," he said. "We needed a final chance to speak to you before the job kicked off, and we hoped he'd take the bait, or at least be distracted enough that I could send you a few texts without him noticing."

"Sorry," Lauren said. "I left my phone inside. I should have messaged you, it's just… I felt like I was suffocating in there. I just had to get out."

Reilly knew that Cam would be listening in, expecting him to scold her, but he decided against it. Her eyes looked hollow, and he wondered if it was anxiety over the drug deal or just a lack of sleep.

"It's okay," he said instead. "It worked out, anyway. We now have some intel that our cartel contact didn't even know."

Lauren leaned against the side of the fire escape, her fingers tight around the rusting metal rail. "Apparently, Cody expects me to work alone, driving a car filled with huge bags of fentanyl. And you and the rest of the Forge brothers want me to double cross the gang that just bought them."

Reilly wanted to reach out and place a comforting hand on her arm, but she was keeping her distance, her arms crossed over her chest.

"Believe it or not, this is actually the best possible setup," he said. "I'd go so far as to say Cody's plan is a blessing. You won't have to worry about any other actors getting in the way. You'll be alone. And once you are, you'll be able to communicate with us."

He paused, fishing the earpiece out of his pocket and laying it on his open palm.

"All you have to do is finish the deal, drive toward wherever it is they want you to go, and put this in as soon as you're away from them."

Lauren plucked the plastic object from his hand, turning it over between her fingers.

"Then what?"

"Then I'll try and intercept you myself," Reilly said firmly. "And as a last resort, El Paso PD will step in. Cameron and I will be contacting them as soon as the deal goes down."

Lauren's face fell.

"I can't do this. The cops won't understand. They'll arrest me," she said, her words tumbling out on top of one another. "Allie said as much. I've committed other drug crimes, and that's just the start–"

"Stop."

"Reilly–"

With a glance over his shoulder, Reilly took a step closer and placed a hand on her shoulder. She flinched, but she didn't pull away.

"FBS has legal help, and we have money. Lots of money. Gabe and the others have committed to protecting you, and that includes any potential tangles with El Paso PD."

Lauren reached up and swiped at her eye with the sleeve of the black hoodie she wore. For the first time since Reilly had met her, she had shed her mask of thick black eyeliner for a more subtle look. Her eyes looked even more striking with only a touch of mascara to highlight them, though he wished that he could stop her from shedding even a single tear.

"Like I said, it's only a last resort. If all goes according to plan, as soon as the money has changed hands and the Iron Prophets have cleared out, Cameron will go for El Pez. We'll deal with Thomas Crown and the rest of his guys later. We need to focus on the cartel boss while he's on American soil."

Lauren let out a shuddering breath. Finally, she nodded.

"Okay. I just hope I can trust you."

Her sorrowful words felt like a knife twisting in his gut. How many men had she trusted who had later hurt her or betrayed her?

"You can," he said. He leaned forward and gave her a soft kiss on the cheek, glad that he had his earpiece turned down low as Cameron yelled at him. "I have to go. But if you just follow the plan, everything is going to be okay. In a few more hours you'll be free. I promise."

CHAPTER
TEN

RAFAEL

Rafael Delgado peered through his binoculars, trying to commit every detail of the man on the fire escape to memory while he was standing relatively still.

Perhaps after today, his *jefe* would finally invest in a decent camera with a long-range zoom feature. He'd more than proven that he deserved better equipment.

Rafael smiled to himself, reaching over with his free hand and digging out a few Cheetos from the bag that sat on the passenger seat of his car.

The next few minutes passed, and he watched as the man–probably hispanic or native American, if he had to guess–leaned over and kissed Lauren Ortega's cheek.

Bingo.

A real kiss would have been better, of course, but it was enough to prove his point.

He had been suspicious of Cody Deller from the start. Nothing about him was impressive, and the fact that he played such a critical role in the Iron Prophets' drug businesses gave him pause.

When he'd learned that Deller had enlisted his street dealer slash small-time mule girlfriend to help run the product, his concern had only grown.

He'd tried to tell El Pez as much, of course, but his warnings had fallen on deaf ears, and he could only say so much to try and convince the man. He knew his place.

But that didn't mean he was going to let his *jefe* and the rest of the cartel walk into a potential trap thanks to the Iron Prophets' incompetence.

And now he had solid proof that they were about to do just that.

He watched, chewing on a mouthful of Cheetos, as the man on the balcony headed down the stairs. He tossed the binoculars onto the seat beside him. They were no use now that the man was in motion, and he was heading in the wrong direction to get a closer look now, anyway.

Dusting the orange residue from his fingers, he picked up one of his several burner phones from where it rested in his cup holder and dialed the familiar number.

"Angelico," El Pez answered after only two rings, "excited for tonight?"

Rafael released a sigh of relief at the sound of the nickname that his *jefe* had bestowed upon him. It sounded like he was in a very good mood. He always dreaded delivering bad news, but maybe this time it would go over better than usual.

Then again, how could he honestly answer El Pez's question?

"I've found something I think I should disclose while we still have time."

The line went silent for several seconds before he heard a sigh on the other end.

"I told you. Crown is in charge of his men, and I trust his judgment."

"I know, *jefe*," he said carefully. "I do not mean any disrespect to Crown or to the Prophets, but there have been rumors–"

"Rumors? There are always rumors," El Pez snapped. "If I lost my cajones every time the girls gossiped, I'd be out of business."

"But this time I've confirmed them myself," he continued, his palm slick with sweat as he gripped the phone. This was not going well, but he had to keep going. El Pez took risks, but he was no fool. Surely he'd see sense.

"I already told you that I didn't trust this Lauren Ortega character that Cody Deller has brought into the job for tonight. At best, she doesn't have the experience. But now I have seen her with my own eyes, cozying up to some guy. I don't think it's the first time."

"What guy?" El Pez demanded.

"I don't know," he admitted. "I only saw him at a distance, but he didn't look like a banger. He was clean cut, good looking, mid thirties. The guys and I have been surveilling the Prophets like you requested, and I figured Cody's apartment needed my personal attention."

The *jefe* sighed. "I suppose so, Angelico."

"Are we going to call off the job?"

El Pez started to chuckle, and Rafael gripped the phone more tightly, forcing himself to keep his mouth shut rather than telling the powerful cartel leader just how naive he was being.

"No way. We're about to make money. A lot of money. It's not the time for any hasty decisions."

"But this guy could be a cop!"

El Pez didn't reply right away.

Rafael grew more anxious with each passing second. In the cartel, respect was everything. He'd served faithfully for years, but if he'd learned anything, it was that ultimately, everybody was replaceable.

Especially those who dared to cross their betters.

"Do you think I'm stupid, Angelico?" he said at last.

"No. Forgive me, *jefe*. I'm just concerned, that's all."

"Just because I'm not going to drop the deal doesn't mean we're not going to act," El Pez said. "The girl is probably just cheating on her boyfriend. But it still reveals bad judgment on said boyfriend's side, no? Like you said, maybe it was foolish for him to choose her to run our fentanyl."

Rafael breathed out a sigh of relief. It seemed that, for the moment, the cartel leader's good mood would continue to hold.

"Yes," he agreed. "There's more to running a solid business than trusting people within the family, blood or otherwise."

"Exactly my thinking, Angelico," El Pez said. "I think we can help the Iron Prophets learn a valuable lesson. They will see just how loyal Cody Deller is when his girl is on the line. See you tonight."

Without another word, he hung up the phone, leaving Rafael smiling from ear to ear.

CHAPTER
ELEVEN

LAUREN

Lauren had never seen so many potholes in her life.

She gritted her teeth as she and Cody bumped along the old highway, making her feel like the tires beneath their old sedan might blow at any moment.

It was annoying, but in truth, she was thankful for the distraction.

"Just think of what the rest of the year will bring for us," her boyfriend was saying from the passenger seat, giving her hand a squeeze.

She was too anxious to decide if his familiar touch was comforting or revolting.

"I know," she said quietly, glad that he had done most of the talking so far. The drive from El Paso toward the site of the deal felt never ending. Already, dusk had fallen, painting the desert horizon in hues of purple and blue.

Lauren stared out the front windshield, looking without taking much in. Soon enough, they'd reach the remote chemical warehouse they were headed toward, and she'd have to face the music.

Somewhere behind them, the other two members of their party were following in a second vehicle. As for where the cartel was coming from, she had no idea, and it made her uneasy.

She fingered the earpiece in her pocket with her free hand, glad that it was far too small for Cody to have noticed it.

She knew that Reilly and Cameron were on their way, but so much could still go wrong. She doubted that her heart would stop racing until everything was over and she was long gone.

"Hey, don't look so worried," Cody was saying, turning from the empty blacktop ahead of them for a moment and catching her eye. "I know you're probably still mad at me, and I deserve it, but things are going to change. I know it. With this money, I'll be able to give you the life you deserve."

She forced herself to smile at him, unable to quell the guilt that rose in her chest at the thought of what she was about to do. Cody was flawed, but who wouldn't be, after the way they'd grown up?

Then again, everyone made choices. Cody had continued to rise within the ranks of the Iron Prophets, seeking more and more control and power.

She'd made similarly bad decisions, so she could hardly judge him any more than she condemned herself, but now, she was choosing something different. And she couldn't let her loyalty to him ruin her chance to break free.

She doubted that FBS was going to give her an escape plan B. This was her shot.

"Just promise me you'll be careful," she said at last, letting go of the earpiece and attempting to fan some of the car's weak air conditioning in the direction of her face. Even at this time of night, the August heat still lingered. "You can't trust anybody."

Cody nodded solemnly, taking his hand from her own and

leading the car in a sharp turn off the asphalt and onto a dirt road that was little more than a track.

She hated how true her words were.

Then again, she wasn't worried about his safety where Reilly, Cameron, or even the police were concerned. Not compared to the cartel, at any rate. They were the people he really had to watch out for.

Finally, up ahead, a cluster of buildings broke the monotonous landscape of rocks and cacti. Neither of them spoke as they bumped along the road, the sun slipping further below the horizon.

Lauren felt a shiver running down her back despite the heat.

Most of the drug dealing she'd done had taken place in public settings, where the chances of being shot or stabbed by her buyer was low.

Here, they'd be completely isolated.

This was the big leagues, and there was no turning back.

REILLY

Reilly yawned as he peered out into the growing darkness, struggling to keep his eyes open. His sleep the night before had been terrible, and he highly doubted that tonight would be any better.

Cameron, on the other hand, looked as though he was going to bounce out of his seat at any moment.

"You good, bro?" Reilly asked, giving him a dirty look as he began tapping his fingers loudly against the metal door of the glove compartment. "You're making me anxious."

"I just wish we'd been able to take a better look around, is all. I hate the feeling of going in blind."

Reilly couldn't argue.

The chemical warehouse was actively used during the day, and he was sure they must have some level of twenty-four-hour security, especially considering that they were clearly working with El Pez's cartel to allow them to conduct business here.

Perhaps they used this facility to synthesize their own drugs, though their contact in Mexico was quite certain that this particular batch of fentanyl had begun its life in Juárez.

In any case, he and Cam hadn't exactly been able to go poking around.

Instead, they'd parked the ancient, rusted truck near the side of a building and sat tight. So far, it seemed they fit right into the landscape.

"You still think our guy's intel is solid? About the site?" he asked instead, peering down at the blank screen of the open laptop in front of him. If they had the location of the hand-off wrong, nothing else would matter.

Cellular service out here was spotty, and the truck didn't have the same signal boosting capabilities as the van they'd been using before. So far, he couldn't see nor hear Lauren, and he could only hope that the equipment she wore was continuing to function properly.

In any case, even if he could see where she and Cody were driving, he doubted he'd be able to confirm they were headed in the direction of the warehouse.

Even in full daylight conditions, the desert had a way of blending together into one endless, bleak landscape.

"This is the place," Cameron said firmly. "Look."

He tore his eyes away from the screen and followed his cousin's gesture. Along the horizon, he could just see a cloud of dust rising, growing in size as it quickly drew closer.

He couldn't decide whether he should be relieved or nervous.

"Well, the cartel is prompt," Reilly said, grabbing the small set of binoculars he'd set in the cupholder between them and trying to get a closer look despite the growing darkness.

"Come on, darkness. We need night vision," Cam grumbled, looking down at the laptop's surveillance screen again, which remained stubbornly blank.

Reilly nodded, tapping the side of his earpiece with his free hand as he continued to watch the approaching cartel vehicles kicking up the desert sand.

"Hey Ben," he said as soon as his cousin acknowledged him. "I think it's time to say our prayers. Location confirmed, cartel arrival confirmed. Also, how're Lauren's feeds looking?"

"Lauren and Cody are en route," Ben replied, his deep, gravelly voice echoing through his skull.

Fortunately, his cousin's equipment–both for receiving and sending data–was much higher tech than either Lauren's or their own. It was a lot easier to set up in their office back in San Antonio rather than out in the middle of nowhere.

"I have El Paso PD on speed dial," Ben continued. "I'll contact them as soon as you nail the big boss."

"DEA?"

"Gabe thinks it's better to let El Paso PD make that call."

Reilly felt a knot of worry in his gut, hoping that Gabe knew what he was doing.

He trusted his oldest cousin's leadership and his judgment, but still, it didn't feel great knowing that he and Cameron were out here in the desert with zero backup, about to be caught up between two criminal organizations that wouldn't hesitate to take them down.

It was risky, but he knew it was the best shot they had to be able to help Lauren–not to mention the fact that right now, their stealth represented a huge advantage.

"All right, they're getting out," Cameron said beside him as he peered through his own binoculars.

"Godspeed," Ben said into his ear. "I'll be quiet for now, but leave the line open so I can hear you."

"Will do."

Cam nodded his agreement and tapped his own earpiece.

Reilly watched as five men emerged from two new white pickups. Three of them wore neat khakis and dress shoes, and the other two wore jeans and sneakers.

"Five guys, Ben," Cam said, not taking his eyes off their quarry.

As the men moved a little closer to where their truck stood, he was able to pick out the cartel members' faces with more detail.

One of them was older than the others. He was tall, with dark black hair, pale brown skin, and eyes so blue that they were visible even in the final minutes of sunlight. There was no mistaking him.

"Visual on El Pez," he said.

It was clear on closer inspection that his clothes were the most expensive out of the three well-dressed men, and Reilly could see the flash of a Rolex on his wrist as he took out his phone and began scrolling.

The two guys in jeans were arrayed around him, weapons holstered at their waists.

"No drugs in the open yet," he said to Ben. He assumed they were probably in the trucks, or perhaps they'd been dropped off at the site beforehand. They'd have to wait and see if they wanted to know for sure.

"Okay, so that's El Pez, and those are his cartel goons," Cameron said, dropping his binoculars for a moment and wiping a sheen of sweat from his brow, "but who are the two white guys? The nerdy looking ones?"

Reilly squinted into the growing darkness, realizing at once what Cameron meant. The only real similarity between them and El Pez were the khakis they all wore. These guys looked like they belonged in a cubicle somewhere, particularly the younger one.

"That guy looks about fifteen," he said.

Cameron nodded. "I'd guess maybe twenty-two, twenty-three, but yeah. I wonder who he is and how he's caught up in this business."

"Maybe he's an apprentice chemist, and the older guy is his boss?"

Cam frowned. "It would make sense, I guess, but it's a little unorthodox for the manufacturers to be so involved in distribution."

Reilly barely heard him.

The laptop screen lit up with a grainy image of the inside of a car.

"Looks like the Iron Prophets are about to roll up," he said, struggling to calm his racing heart. Lauren was close now, and that meant the danger to her had just become all the more real.

He set the binoculars down and leaned back in his chair, forcing himself to take several breaths.

"Lord Jesus, please guide us through this," Cameron was saying beside him. "Grant us Your strength, Your mercy, and Your wisdom. Please protect us, our informant, and any other lives that can be reasonably safeguarded. In your name we pray, Amen."

"Amen," Reilly echoed.

CHAPTER
TWELVE

LAUREN

"What? The reception here sucks. Okay. Yeah, she's ready," Cody said into his phone, keeping one hand firmly on the steering wheel as they continued down the narrow dirt road. Blessedly, it had smoothed out a little, and the smaller bumps no longer made Lauren's teeth hurt. "I told you, she's solid. No! I said she's solid! Okay. See you in five."

As he hung up the phone, Lauren glanced through the rear windshield, where she could see the headlights of a car as it kicked up dust against the deepening twilight.

Thomas Crown was in it, probably in the backseat, being chauffeured.

Dez would be driving. She couldn't help but to think of his girlfriend Lily, ever loyal, who would probably be by her phone all night waiting for news. Lauren hoped he'd make it out of this unscathed, especially for the sake of their twins. Assuming he and Lily somehow got their lives together and regained more stable custody of them.

Guilt clutched at her throat as she watched Cody navigating a curve in the road, the cluster of buildings up ahead looming closer with each passing moment.

She wanted him to walk away from this, too.

She sighed. A part of her would always love him, but her concern went deeper than that.

She couldn't bear the thought that he might never turn aside from his present course in search of a better life. But for the past few years, he'd only driven himself more deeply into the operations of the Iron Prophets. It didn't give her much hope.

Reilly would probably tell her to pray for him. Maybe he had a point.

Before she could consider the thought further, however, Cody reached over and rested a hand on her shoulder. The rumbling tires went quiet as he pulled their sedan to a stop. The long, lonely road had ended in nothing but a patch of dirt.

"So, this is it," he said, gesturing toward the complex of warehouse buildings that now surrounded them. "Looks like the cartel is already here. We'll sit tight for now."

Lauren didn't need to be convinced.

She peered out the passenger window, watching the men who now stood talking in the middle of the makeshift courtyard.

"Looks like they stuck to the crew size that Crown agreed to," Cody said under his breath. "Five men to our four. Unless they're hiding snipers or something."

Lauren peered up at one of the taller buildings that stood nearby, shuddering as she tried to spot anyone who might be lurking in the darkened windows. She certainly hoped the cartel had kept their word.

The men were all facing her, but in the gloom it was difficult to get a very good look at their faces. One, however, stood out.

El Pez.

Even if she hadn't recognized his face from the evening news, it was clear by the way he carried himself that he was in charge.

Another shiver slid down her back.

The man was known for his brutality. He didn't reserve violence for those who opposed the interests of the cartel. If anything, he was even more harsh toward anyone on his own side that dared to cross him.

Cody's phone rang again, disrupting her anxious thoughts. She forced herself to breathe in and out. Reilly and Cameron were either here already, or on their way, and she had to believe that they'd keep her safe.

Once again, she toyed with the earpiece hidden in her pocket. In that moment, she'd give anything just to hear Reilly's reassuring voice. Or better yet, to be close to him, inhaling the scent of his cologne.

Safe.

Not that now was the time to think of just how badly she'd wanted to kiss him earlier that day.

"All right, baby girl," her boyfriend said, hanging up and jabbing his phone into his pocket. She watched out the window as one of the cartel men–this one dressed in simple jeans and a t-shirt–looked over at their car, his expression unreadable.

Now that night had fallen, several huge outdoor lamps had switched on, casting pools of yellow light across the expanse of sand. Outside of their reach, however, the shadows looked darker and more menacing than before.

"Dez says they have the cash ready," Cody continued. "When Crown hands it to El Pez, Dez and I will load this car with the fentanyl."

He paused for a moment, glancing at her expectantly until she nodded.

"Anyway, once that's done, Dez, Crown, and I will head back to El Paso, and you'll drive to the drop. Got it?"

She nodded again. On the drive over, she'd already memorized the address of the abandoned rest stop where two more members of the Iron Prophets would be waiting for her. One would load the drugs onto a truck and torch the sedan, and the other would drive her back home, assuming the coast was clear.

Of course, none of that would happen.

Unless Reilly and Cameron failed.

She pushed the possibility aside. "So I just wait here, then?"

"You got it. It'll just be a few minutes, and you'll be gone. You can do this, babe."

Before she knew how to react, Cody had leaned over toward the passenger seat, his lips crushing hers in a desperate kiss. She had no choice but to return it, grasping the back of his neck as though she wanted nothing more than to have him close to her.

When it was over, she forced herself to smile at him.

"Be safe out there, okay?"

He caught her eye for several long seconds before getting out of the car and closing the door behind him.

She watched as he approached the members of the cartel, shaking hands with each of the men in turn, as though this was nothing more than a normal business meeting. Good. If they could keep everything civil, things might turn out okay.

Still, she wished that she could reach out to Reilly and find out what exactly they were planning, now that they had a lay of the land and presumably eyes on El Pez.

Before she could think about it further, however, Cody raised a hand in her direction, gesturing for her to come toward him.

She froze as her heart began to pound against her ribcage, unsure what she was supposed to do. He'd specifically told her to wait in the car. This wasn't part of the plan.

Was it the cartel who demanded her presence?

She tried to look at El Pez and his men, but they stood near the edges of the pools of light, leaving their faces mostly obscured in shadow.

Cody's expression was clear, however–she had to get out of the car.

Now.

She made a last minute decision to remove the earpiece from her pocket and hide it in her sock. Now that she'd be in close proximity to the cartel, she was taking no chances of being found out.

She opened the car door and got out, forcing her feet to propel her toward where the men stood. Her only hope was that Reilly and his cousin were seeing everything she saw, and that they had a plan if things went south. There was nothing else she could do but to comply, just as Reilly had told her.

As she stepped into the light next to where Cody stood, she was surprised to see El Pez striding toward her, hand outstretched, with a friendly smile on his face.

He said something in Spanish, and one of the men in jeans translated.

"The *jefe* wanted to meet the person the Iron Prophets have entrusted to deliver our product," he said in clear, accented English. "Just a precaution. El Paso PD would love to get their hands on it."

Cody pressed a hand against the small of her back, urging her forward.

She kept her head up as she approached, not wanting any of the men to know just how terrified she was.

Despite the calm, indifferent looks on their faces, she couldn't seem to quell her fear.

"*Gracias*, Angelico," she heard El Pez saying softly to the man who had translated his words.

At last she reached him, extending her own hand as she racked her brain for the correct Spanish words to offer a respectful greeting. Despite her grandmother's attempts to teach Lauren their native language, she was far from fluent.

"*Buenas tardes, señor. Es un honor conocerte.*"

She plastered a smile on her face as his large hand clasped her own.

His own friendly smile fell away in an instant.

She cried out as he grabbed her wrist with his other hand, his grip turning to iron as he twisted her arm and yanked her toward him.

Cody was shouting something, but she couldn't comprehend the words.

All she could understand was the feeling of the cold knife pressed against her throat.

CHAPTER
THIRTEEN

REILLY

R eilly peered through his night-vision goggles, trying to keep track of who was who despite the fact that everyone outside was now cast in green. At last, the sun had sunk completely below the horizon, only to be replaced with the glow of artificial lights that made it almost as difficult to see as it had been at dusk.

He squinted at the group of people, his gaze sweeping over them as he tried to count how many were present.

"Wait," Cameron said beside him. "I think the Prophets are getting out."

Reilly heard Cody's voice coming through over Lauren's recording device, but his words were too muffled to make out.

He directed his gaze outside the ring of lights, where the two cars carrying Lauren and the other gang members had parked. The two of them watched as Cody, Thomas Crown, and their other associate, Dez, walked up to the El Pez.

"What're you seeing, guys?" Ben asked quietly in his ear.

Reilly tuned his cousins out as Cameron gave a quick

update, trying to figure out what the men were discussing. Unfortunately, he didn't know how to read lips.

A few moments later, he watched as Cody stepped out of the circle of light he'd stood under. In the shadows, Reilly could see that he was raising a hand in the direction of his car.

"What's he doing?" Cameron asked.

"No idea. Keep eyes on El Pez," Reilly commanded, gesturing toward the rest of the men.

He turned his attention to the car where Lauren now sat alone.

On the camera feed, he watched as she turned toward the window, clearly catching sight of Cody.

He swung his field of vision back in the man's direction. Sure enough, he was waving. Beckoning for her to get out of the car.

"No, no, no," he muttered under his breath, "don't get out."

Cameron continued to stare at the circle of men. "What's happening, Reilly?"

His heart was pounding in his chest so loudly that he barely heard his cousin's question.

He watched as Lauren took the earpiece out of her pocket and shoved it into the top of her sock.

Before he could think of what to do, she was getting out of the car, and walking toward Cody.

And toward the cartel.

"She's getting out," Cameron said, realization dawning as she walked into his own field of view. "Why is she getting out?"

Reilly ignored him, trying to divert his attention between the night vision goggles and the laptop screen.

Lauren walked until she stood beside Cody, and paused there for only a moment before continuing forward.

El Pez had extended a hand for her to shake. Reilly could see the man's mouth moving, but the microphone picked up only snatches of Spanish. The wind had picked up slightly, and the sensitive equipment was now capturing each whisper of the breeze.

Cameron swore from the passenger seat. "What are they saying, Ben? I can't hear a thing."

"It's the wind, man," Ben answered over their earpieces. "I don't know what's going on. I'm trying to see."

"We need to get closer," Reilly cut in, glancing over at the heavier guns that rested in the small backseat of the rusted-out truck before returning his gaze to Lauren's body camera feed. "I don't know if we can wait for the exchange. She shouldn't–"

Before he could say anything else, the image on the laptop shifted, and he heard Lauren let out a stifled cry of fear.

He saw a flash of skin, a brief image of clothing, and then nothing but darkness.

Reilly heard Cam swear again as he desperately tried to peer through the night vision goggles, trying to figure out what he was seeing.

"Not good, not good," Ben was saying over the earpiece.

Lauren was standing in front of El Pez, unable to move as his thick arms encircled her. He began yanking her backward, out of the circle of light and toward the shadows that lay beyond.

In the green gleam of his night vision, Reilly saw the flash of a knife.

He dropped the goggles and lunged for the nearest weapon behind him, but before he could get his fingers around the gunstock, he felt Cameron's fingers clamping around his shoulder and dragging him back.

"Stop it!" Cam half-shouted before remembering where they were and lowering his voice. "Right now. Stop it."

Reilly tried to shake his cousin off, but Cam only held on tighter.

"Just think. Please."

He made one final attempt to yank himself free of Cam's grip before letting his muscles relax. They might only have seconds to act. Fighting with his only ally was a foolish waste of time.

"That scumbag has her," he choked out instead, picking up the goggles and staring out the window. "We need to go."

"No," Cameron snapped. "She's an informant, Reilly. This was always a risk. You knew that, and more importantly, she knew that."

He felt his jaw going tight as he tried to breathe. It took every ounce of self control he had not to reach for the gun again and rush out into the desert, backup or no backup.

"You can't let your attachment to her blind you," Ben added over his earpiece. "We need to wait. And think."

"I can't just let him hurt her," Reilly said, trying not to shout and alert the men outside to their presence.

"There has to be a reason El Pez is threatening her," Cameron was saying, shaking his head as he watched the scene through his own goggles. "He probably knows she's double-crossing him. He must have found out somehow."

So far, no one seemed to be doing much of anything, but Reilly could see the desperation in Lauren's eyes. The gusts of wind had obscured the sounds of her breathing, but otherwise, he was sure he would have heard it over the microphone she wore.

She was terrified.

"If you jump in and act without thinking, you could make things worse," Ben reminded him. "Much worse."

He heard a few words being picked up by Lauren's microphone. A moment later, he could see Cody taking a couple of steps forward and raising his gun.

"Watch and listen," Cameron said firmly, reaching over and turning up the speakers connected to the laptop as loud as they could go. "We need to get our footing before we move in."

Reilly swallowed the bile that had risen in his throat.

They were right.

If El Pez didn't know who she was working with already, he would threaten her with violence until he found out.

And if Lauren talked, it wouldn't just be the cartel she had to worry about.

She'd be surrounded by enemies on both sides.

LAUREN

If the knife moved even an inch, she was dead.

Lauren forced herself to breathe more slowly, trying to slow her racing heart. Panicking wouldn't help.

She tried to glance around in search of Reilly, but she didn't dare move her head.

In front of her, she watched as Cody took a couple steps toward El Pez, his eyes flashing with fury.

Despite the gravity of the situation, she couldn't help but to feel a slight glimmer of relief. By the look of it, this wasn't some sort of setup by the Iron Prophets. She could see by the look on Dez and Crown's faces that they were just as surprised as she was.

"What's going on here?" Cody barked at El Pez, reaching into his waistband and taking hold of his gun. He raised it until it pointed directly at the cartel boss's head.

"No, don't," Lauren said quickly, her voice becoming a squeak of panic as she felt the knife pressing more firmly against her skin, close enough that she feared El Pez had drawn blood.

She heard Dez swear, raising his hands over his head in surrender, though no one seemed to be paying him any particular attention.

"Cool it, Deller," Thomas Crown snapped, taking a step toward Cody.

Lauren could hear nothing but the sound of her own racing heart.

She kept hoping that Reilly and Cameron were going to emerge from the shadows with machine guns, gaining control of the situation in an instant like heroes in a spy movie, but she could see nothing but darkness surrounding the pools of lamplight.

Cody kept the gun raised for several long breaths, his hand shaking as he met Lauren's eyes. She was afraid to speak again, but she hoped he understood by her stare that all this would accomplish would be getting them both killed.

With the exception of the twenty-something guy in khakis, El Pez's men looked totally calm, as though this whole fiasco was a routine occurrence. Perhaps it was.

She heard the cartel boss clearing his throat at her ear, his grip on the knife unwavering. To her surprise, he was speaking English.

"I don't like how you run your business," he said, gesturing toward Thomas Crown with his free hand. "You need to be more careful who you trust. A lot more careful."

Cody lowered the gun slightly as he looked over at his boss, confusion shadowing his features. A moment later, however, he stepped closer to them, his grip tightening on the weapon.

"We can talk about this after you let her go," he growled, no longer meeting Lauren's eyes.

Now, he was staring straight at the murderous man who held her hostage.

She wanted to yell at him, but at the same time, renewed guilt threatened to overwhelm her. Despite all of the times he had hurt her, both emotionally and physically, it was clear that he did care about her.

And she was okay with leaving him deep in the heart of the Iron Prophets, so long as she escaped.

She felt like a terrible person.

Not that it mattered now.

She felt the plastic of the earpiece she'd hidden in her sock jabbing against the side of her foot, taunting her.

Reilly wasn't coming to save the day. Whatever the cause of her current predicament, it was obvious that whatever deal she had with Forge Brothers Security was null and void.

It wasn't what they signed up for, and as angry as she was at herself for trusting them, she could hardly blame them for not wanting to get themselves killed.

"Please, *señor*," Thomas Crown said, striding forward until he'd stepped into the path of Cody's gun. "My colleague will put the gun down. Let's talk."

Lauren could no longer see her boyfriend's face, but to her relief, he stuck the weapon back into his pants, defeated.

El Pez began to chuckle behind her, his tobacco-breath puffing into her cheek.

"Smarter than you look, no?"

Cody took his place beside Crown, but didn't reply to the man's insult.

Dez was a few feet away from them, eyeing the other cartel men with suspicion, though none of them had moved so much as an inch. While the Iron Prophets had been thrown for a loop, clearly the cartel had been planning this from the start.

"I don't think I need to tell you that loyalty is everything in our business," he continued. "Wouldn't you agree?"

Thomas nodded.

"So, you can understand my concern when you are entrusting five hundred grand worth of fentanyl to a girl who can't even manage to be faithful to her partner."

Lauren sucked in a breath.

No.

Cody shrunk back as though he'd been slapped, letting the gun hang loosely against his side as he cast his furious gaze in her direction.

"It's not true!" she said, ignoring the threat of the blade against her throat. "Cody, he's–"

"I'm lying, is that it?" El Pez asked calmly, turning to face Crown once again. "Thomas, you know how I do business. I don't make wild accusations."

"It's–it's between them, right?" Dez said, his voice shaking as he addressed the others. "I mean, if she's cheating, I think Cody can handle his own girl."

Cody said nothing, but by the way his neck was going red with rage, she had a feeling that his idea of handling it would involve his fists–though she'd rather take a few punches to the head if the alternative was having her throat slit.

The other cartel members looked over at El Pez, waiting to hear what he'd say. Lauren held her breath, unsure what to hope for.

Instead, it was Crown who spoke.

He shook his head slowly.

"No, Dez," he said. "El Pez is right. It's about trust. If Lauren is sleeping around with someone on the side, how do we know she hasn't told him about the deal? How can we trust anything she says?"

"No, please," Lauren tried again, struggling against El Pez's iron grip. "I didn't. There's no one. No one knows anything, I swear."

"Hmm," El Pez hummed, his breath whispering against her ear. "I'm curious what *el novio* thinks."

"I had my suspicions," Cody said. "I should have acted on them sooner. Forgive me, *señor*."

Lauren stared at him.

All of his talk about family, about loyalty–it had all been nothing but a lie. He didn't believe her. He wouldn't even give her the benefit of the doubt.

"Cody, please," Lauren begged. She felt hot, salty tears spilling over her cheeks and onto her lips. "It's a mistake–I didn't–"

Before she could get the words out, she felt El Pez's lips pressing against her neck, his tongue licking at her sweat as he kissed her trembling flesh.

"Shut up," he said as he pulled away.

She clamped her mouth shut. If she tried to talk, she was afraid she might be sick. The intimate feeling of his touch was almost worse than the pressure of the blade.

"Ms. Ortega here will make a nice thank you gift for a lawyer friend of mine who took the time to come all this way in person," he said. "Unless you object?"

Cody stared at her as he spat on the ground.

"I don't care what you do with her."

Lauren wished that she could close her ears as he added a few choice words about the kind of woman she was.

The tears were falling freely now, leaving dots of mud in the sand at her feet.

Without Reilly, Cody was the only hope she had of staying alive, and now that hope was gone, too. Even Dez would no longer meet her eyes. He wasn't a monster, but whether he believed their accusations or not, he wasn't about to cross her boyfriend, let alone the cartel.

"Listen, El Pez," Crown said, raising a hand. "I'm in charge of my crew. Mistakes were made, as you say, and I apologize. I'll run the product myself this time. Next time, I'll choose my crew more carefully."

"Done," El Pez said. "Now, Deller, you'd be wise to go get out of my face and feel lucky that all you got was a warning. Go."

Cody refused to meet her eyes as he nodded toward the boss, turned on his heel, and strode off toward their vehicle.

A few seconds later, she heard the rumble of the ignition, and the group went silent as they listened to him driving away from the cluster of warehouses.

"Now that that's over with, I think you boys need to load the product, no?"

The cartel men in jeans fell in beside Thomas Crown and Dez, and the men began walking toward the other car, their bodies disappearing into the shadows as they left the yellow glow of the lights.

"I'll be there soon," El Pez called to their backs. "Be ready."

A moment later, Lauren felt the knife pulling away from her neck, and she wasted no time.

She began to kick and scream, trying with every ounce of her strength to get El Pez to let go of her, but it was no use. The man was far stronger than he looked, and worse, the two nerdy-looking men were still with him.

Still, she kept trying, until finally, she managed to get her arm free of the man's grip. She raised it and struck out blind, feeling pain in her knuckles as she realized her fist had collided with the side of the man's head.

He caught hold of her wrist at once, twisting it back as he raised his free hand. She winced, expecting a slap to the face at minimum, but none came.

Instead, El Pez leaned toward her ear, his whisper so quiet that the other men could not hear it.

"They call me "the fish", *señora*," he said. "Do you know why?"

She shook her head.

He pulled out the knife again, holding it in front of her face for a moment before lowering it and pointing the tip at the strip of exposed skin along her belly. He pressed it against her flesh, and she fought to keep herself from shaking as he gently traced a line from side to side.

He chuckled, his hot breath making her clench her neck in disgust. "It's kind of a silly name, really. They should call me the fisherman. It's me who does the gutting."

CHAPTER
FOURTEEN

REILLY

Reilly rested his head against the seat of the truck, closing his eyes as he replayed what he had just heard in his mind.

The conversation had come over their surveillance equipment in snippets, but he got the gist of it.

El Pez had told the members of the Iron Prophets that Lauren was disloyal, and they had believed him.

She was in big, big trouble.

Ben was talking to Cameron over their earpieces, but he had stopped listening. As the vital seconds and minutes raced by, they were still trying to figure out how to get a clearer image and a better sound on Lauren's equipment. The reception had only gotten worse as the men had headed off toward the shadows near one of the warehouses.

Cam wouldn't let him leave the truck, and he had good reasons why. If Reilly gave away the fact that she was an informant too soon, he would succeed in nothing but getting her killed.

A scream sounded over the speakers, louder than any of the cries that had come before it.

Cameron dropped the cable he'd been fiddling with, putting a finger to his lips, though Reilly was hardly going to interrupt the crackling sound coming through Lauren's microphone.

He leaned toward the speakers, listening for more, but there was nothing. The screen was dark, though he couldn't tell if it was because she had walked into the dark or because the camera was malfunctioning.

He no longer cared. He had to get to her.

"Cameron, come on," he nearly shouted, pounding his fist against the steering wheel.

"They don't suspect we're here," his cousin snapped back at him, jabbing a finger toward the window. "We should be thanking God right now. We still have the element of surprise."

"They think she's cheating," Reilly pleaded. "We don't even know where she is or what the other guys in her gang are doing. I need to go in. Come on!"

He heard Ben's gravelly voice scolding him over his earpiece, but Cam said nothing else, turning back to the laptop and clicking around on the video settings.

It was no use.

He leaned back again, trying to offer a prayer to Jesus, but he couldn't get even his own thoughts straight as his heart continued to pound in his chest.

All he could hear were her screams, echoing in his mind again and again.

Minutes passed, but to Reilly, it felt as though time was crawling along by the hour.

"Look, I've got something," Cameron said at last.

He opened his eyes and leaned forward, searching the laptop screen.

His cousin was right.

The speakers offered nothing but static, but he could see something. Lauren was inside one of the buildings, stumbling down a hallway behind the two well-dressed men who had come with El Pez. There was light.

He looked out the window of the truck.

Sure enough, one of the warehouses now had several lights on in its first-floor windows.

"I don't see the Iron Prophets," Ben pointed out. "They're probably back at the car, assuming the cartel is still letting the deal go through."

Reilly nodded, forgetting that his cousin couldn't see him. Through the bits and pieces of conversation they'd picked up, it sounded like El Pez hadn't been willing to lose out on his money over Lauren's apparent disloyalty.

For all Lauren's insistence that the Iron Prophets were a family, it seemed that Cody, Dez, and Crown had seen things differently when it came time to sacrifice her to save their own skins.

"We know where they are. We can sneak up on them," Reilly said, watching as two more lights turned on in the building outside. On the screen of the laptop, he could see Lauren continuing forward. She was clearly being pushed, but at least she was still able to move under her own power. That was something.

"We will wait until we know for sure what's going down, especially with the drugs," Cam said firmly. "We're not going to be careless with our lives for the sake of an informant."

"Lauren—"

"Lauren made choices," Cam said, his blue eyes sharp and determined in the dim light of the truck's cab. "Just like all of us have. You're too close to this, Reilly. Gabe should have pulled you out long before now."

"Well, it's too late for that," Ben chimed in, releasing a heavy sigh.

Reilly forced down the hateful words that he wanted so desperately to say.

He knew they were right.

In this business, they had no choice but to be clear headed, logical, and careful. There was no room for relationships that jeopardized that.

It was just as the Bible said. The heart was deceitful, and it couldn't be trusted.

But in that moment, he struggled to care about the admonitions of the Lord.

How much time did Lauren have left?

LAUREN

As El Pez shoved her down the twisting hallways of the warehouse, Lauren tried her best to focus on keeping her bearings. No one was coming to save her, and as unlikely as it was that she'd be able to escape, any attempt would end before it started if she couldn't even find her way out of the building.

The place was huge, with dozens of doors, most of them without numbers or any other markings. A few had signs denoting that dangerous chemicals or poisons were stored within, however, and she hoped that meant that most of the others were probably offices.

Hopefully, offices with windows that would lead outside if she failed to find a door to exit from.

As El Pez urged her to move faster, she looked up at the other two men walking ahead of them. Now that she could see them in the light, she realized that they looked much less out of place inside the warehouse than they had outside of it.

She had a feeling that they both were used to working from an air-conditioned office rather than in the middle of the desert. She wondered if the older of the two was the lawyer that El Pez had mentioned giving her to as a 'gift'.

She shuddered at the thought of the man touching her, but

at the moment, she was a lot more afraid of the cartel boss who currently had her in his grip. At least this guy didn't look particularly frightening.

Then again, El Pez had looked downright friendly when she'd first shook his hand.

At last, they came to a stop at one of the doors.

There was nothing to differentiate it from any of the others, but she lingered for a few extra seconds before walking through it, taking in every detail that she could.

Though she knew hope had become futile, she figured that somewhere, Reilly and his security company might still be watching her camera feed. If nothing else, maybe they'd be able to track down her body for her grandmother's sake when all of this was over.

She shivered as she took a seat in one of the desk chairs at the prodding of El Pez.

"Wait here," he said, turning to the other two men. "I'm going to find a better place to stash the girl until it's time to leave."

Lauren's head swam.

Leave?

She didn't like the sound of that, but she shouldn't have been surprised. If the cartel planned to keep her as some kind of sex slave, she'd probably end up somewhere across the Mexican border, not here outside of El Paso.

For the first time that night, the younger man spoke.

"She'll probably cause less trouble for you if you let her stay in here with us, *señor*."

El Pez paused, his hand resting on the back of her chair.

For the first time since she'd been taken hostage, she wasn't being restrained, but her relative freedom was of little use to her now. The man still had a knife, and she was outnumbered.

No. If she was going to try anything, she'd have to hope there'd be a better opportunity.

El Pez switched over to Spanish once again, and to her surprise, the older man spoke to him in perfect Spanish of his own.

She struggled to make out every word, but she caught the gist of it. They were talking about what to do with her, and the older man said something about 'Chase' being 'young and soft'.

She caught the eye of the younger man, taking in his neatly pressed dress shirt and neatly-creased khakis. He looked even younger than she'd first thought. It was possible he was still in college.

Chase.

Perhaps he was the reasonable one of the three, though with company like El Pez, that wasn't saying much.

"Maybe he has a point after all, boss," the older man said, getting out of the chair he'd been sitting in and taking a few steps toward Lauren. His eyes were dark and small, and she could tell by the lines surrounding them that the man had to be in his late fifties, perhaps older.

When he reached her chair, he bent down until his gaze met her own, taking hold of her chin in his large fingers.

She didn't shy away. She'd been in the game long enough to know that with men like him, showing fear was always the wrong move.

"If it's all right with our friend El Pez here, I'm willing to make you a deal."

The cartel boss chuckled again, sending fresh shivers of terror down her spine. If she somehow got out of this, the man's laugh would haunt her dreams for the rest of her life.

"I told you, she's all yours," he said. "A gift, for coming all this way. I was planning to buy you a nice bottle of tequila, but she's better."

"I'll say," the man said, looking at her hungrily. "In that case, here's my offer. You stay here and be a good girl for me now, and I'll be good to you when I get you back to my place. How does that sound?"

Lauren's palms were damp as she clutched the bottom of the office chair, every bit of her energy focused on maintaining control.

She wanted nothing more than to spit in the pig's face, preferably followed by gouging his eyes out with her thumbs.

Instead, she let her eyes fall away a little, looking toward the ground as though she'd finally submitted.

"It sounds like a deal I can live with, sir," she choked out.

She could see Chase staring at her, his eyebrows lifted as he shuffled from foot to foot. Clearly, he wasn't used to this.

Maybe he'd be useful after all.

But all of her hopes rested on her staying in this room, rather than being tied up alone in some utility closet before being dragged out to a car and driven toward the border.

Several long seconds passed.

El Pez was quiet, though she could feel the whisper of his breath on the top of her head.

Finally, the older man released her chin.

"Agreed."

He got to his feet and dusted invisible dirt from his knees with his hands.

"You don't need to worry, honey," he added, the side of his mouth curling up in a smirk. "I'm sure a gang girl like you is used to a certain type of client. Compared to them, I'll be a gentleman."

She forced herself to nod, though she was sure every bit of her disgust was displayed on her face.

No point in telling him that, so far, she'd managed to avoid that particular line of work.

El Pez stepped out from behind the chair and pulled a gun from a holster at his belt, holding out the butt toward the older man.

"If she tries anything, shoot her," he commanded. "I have plenty more where she came from."

The man took the gun and El Pez headed out of the room without another word, slamming the door behind him.

CHAPTER
FIFTEEN

EL PEZ

E l Pez strode down the hall of the warehouse, shaking his head.

The boy, Chase, might prove to be a problem.

But according to his team, he was trustworthy, and would be an asset to the cartel's American legal team once they fully trained him.

Despite his misgivings, he wasn't going to make a big deal out of nothing. He understood better than most the importance of grooming, at least when it was possible. Getting them young was the best way to ensure total loyalty.

As it was, he wished the job had simply gone off exactly as planned.

As he'd told his lawyer, he had much more beautiful, cleaner girls to offer back at his compound in Juárez. It would have certainly been less trouble, but at least he'd made the best of a less-than-ideal situation.

He scrunched his nose as he glanced up at the various office doors, looking for the room where he'd first met with the owners of the chemical company that used this warehouse. The whole place smelled like feet.

At last, he found the room he was looking for and went inside, sinking down into a cracked leather armchair and pulling out his phone from his pocket.

Missed calls from his wife, of course.

He ignored them, instead looking at the time.

They still had at least an hour before their accomplice at the border would begin his shift, and several hours of leeway after that.

Still, he couldn't help but to feel rushed after the evening's excitement. Hopefully, his men would manage to load the drugs without further incident.

He shoved the phone back into his khakis, rubbing at his temples.

All he wanted was a cigarette, but he'd wait.

The time to relax would come soon enough.

He just had to reach the border.

CHAPTER
SIXTEEN

LAUREN

There was no clock on the wall, and Lauren had left her phone back in the car.

Both of the men who were sitting across from her were wearing watches, but she wasn't about to ask them how much time had passed.

Now that El Pez had gone, she'd been given a little more freedom to move. She leaned back in the office chair, surprised at just how weak and shaky her entire body felt.

Despite the gun that the older man held in his lap, ready to use on her at a moment's notice, her adrenaline was long gone, leaving only exhaustion behind.

Even if she felt up to running, where could she go?

She'd had plenty of time to examine the room, and nothing she'd found was particularly encouraging.

There were three doors. One led to a bathroom. The other, she wasn't sure about, but by its location she assumed it was probably a closet. The third one, the one that they had come through, led out to the maze of hallways, but she doubted she'd reach it without being shot. In any case, she had no idea who might be waiting outside.

There were a couple windows she could fit through, but that option was even less appealing. If she somehow managed to run out into the desert without being fired upon, which was a big 'if', she'd die of thirst before ever finding help. The drive from El Paso had been a long one, and the rural area surrounding the city wasn't exactly known for its vast population.

She lowered her head into her hands and closed her eyes as memories washed over her.

She imagined herself as a little girl in a thrift-store dress, kneeling in church next to her grandmother after her mother had been sent off to jail yet again.

As much as she'd always fidgeted in the pew and complained about the homily, she'd been happy there. She'd been safe, and she'd been loved.

A more recent memory surfaced before she could push it away.

Reilly standing in front of her on the balcony of her grubby old building, pressing his lips to her cheek.

Promising her that she was going to be free.

Tears stung at her eyes.

She didn't doubt that he'd wanted to help her, but in the end, when things had gone wrong, he'd chosen his own safety over protecting her.

She knew that she would have done the same, but that didn't change the hollow ache she felt inside.

She'd let herself believe that his care for her went beyond their mutual self-interest.

What a fool she'd been.

If even God didn't want her, a man like Reilly Forge certainly had no reason to.

It was a stupid hope to have clung to for so long, and she had no one but herself to blame.

"I gotta use the can," the older man said from across the room. She lifted her head, watching as he strode toward the bathroom door and went inside.

The younger man looked up at her, his face revealing nothing but sympathy, but she wouldn't allow herself to believe that it was genuine compassion she saw on display. She doubted the man would say no to his superiors if they offered her or any other woman to him for the taking.

"I'm Chase, by the way," he said, his voice quiet enough not to carry into the bathroom.

She ignored him.

"I didn't think this would happen, you know," he continued. "El Pez was having some problems with his legal team in Mexico, so he called in his American team to oversee some last minute contracts the cartel has with the Iron Prophets."

He paused, gesturing toward the bathroom door. She heard a toilet flush, followed by the sound of the sink running.

"My boss—one of the partners at my firm—dragged me along. That's all I knew before coming here."

Despite her distrust, Lauren was curious. But before she could pry for more information, she heard the bathroom door creaking open.

To her horror, the lawyer didn't return to his chair.

Instead he walked toward her, returning the gun to his freshly-washed hands as he stopped about six inches in front of where she sat.

He said nothing for several long seconds as he looked down at her, his eyes lingering on her chest.

"What do you want?" she asked, no longer bothering to try and sound polite now that El Pez had left.

"Oh, just examining the merchandise," he said nonchalantly. "Thinking about later tonight. I can give you something to keep you awake and full of energy. Or maybe I'll let you sleep while I do the work. What do you think, honey?"

He leaned closer, his empty eyes boring into her own.

She could no longer contain the rage that was boiling inside of her.

Before he could react, she spit in his face.

She expected him to shrink back, but instead he only laughed, wiping at his eye and cheek with the back of his hand.

"Look at that, Chase," he said, looking over his shoulder toward the younger man. "This is why I have a thing for latina girls. They always have some fight in 'em."

She met Chase's eyes, and for a moment, it seemed he would get to his feet and tell the older man to back off.

Instead, he looked at the ground.

She said nothing as the lawyer transferred the gun to his left hand, letting the barrel rest on her shoulder as he stroked her hair with his right, as gentle as could be.

"Don't worry. We'll be on our way soon enough."

Lauren swallowed the tears that threatened to break forth again.

Chase may not be a total psychopath like the rest of them, but otherwise, he was useless.

Reilly and the rest of Forge Brothers Security had abandoned her.

She closed her eyes, trying to stop her body from shaking.

All those years ago at church, her *abuelita* had promised her that with God, she'd never be alone, no matter what her mother or anyone else did. The fallen world they inhabited could take away almost anything from her, but if she leaned on Jesus Christ, her soul would be safe in His hands.

She'd stopped believing in that fairytale years ago. But in that moment, she realized that she truly had nothing left to lose.

She was alone, more alone than she ever had been before.

As the older man stroked at her hair, petting her like she was nothing more than a dog, she began to pray.

She felt foolish at first, but as the seconds turned into minutes, the cool smoothness of the gun against the skin of her neck only strengthened her resolve.

If God was out there, if He was listening, He was going to hear her now.

He had to.

CHAPTER
SEVENTEEN

REILLY

"Okay, I see the product," Cam said, pulling Reilly out of his panicked thoughts.

Finally.

He rolled down the window of the ancient truck, willing to take the risk of drawing attention to himself so long as it gave him a better view.

Cam made no comment, but he was sure his cousin wasn't thrilled.

There was no point in pretending to be calm or rational any more. His regrets had become almost physically painful, like a constant ache pressing against his skull from the inside out.

He never should have allowed Lauren to take part in this operation. If she'd never met him, she'd probably still be sitting in her car in relative safety, waiting as the bags of fentanyl were loaded.

Now, she had been taken hostage, and as far as he knew, she might only have minutes left.

Assuming she was still alive.

Forcing the terrible thought of her potential death from his mind, he pressed his night-vision goggles to his face.

He watched as El Pez's cronies loaded the drugs onto a couple of hand trucks, with the remaining members of the Iron Prophets standing nearby, watching.

"We need to call it in," Cam said a moment later. "Now that the original plan is out the window, we're gonna need firepower if we want to thwart the deal."

Reilly shook his head, continuing to watch as a second batch of drugs was loaded into the trunk of the car that Thomas Crown and Dez had rolled up in.

"If El Paso and the DEA roll up, Lauren's dead," he said firmly.

Cam said nothing for a moment, and Reilly reluctantly turned to face him.

Surely, his cousin knew that he wasn't going to put her life on the line for the sake of stopping a drug sale.

"It's not worth it, Cam," he added.

His cousin pressed his fingers to his temples, deliberating.

He wasn't heartless, and Reilly was counting on that fact.

"You're right," he said finally. "I don't want her getting–"

Just then, Ben's voice sounded over their comms.

"Turn up the volume, I've got ears again," he said excitedly.

Reilly ripped the goggles off his head, nearly lunging for the speakers hooked up to the laptop, but Cameron beat him to it.

The screen had gone stubbornly blank once more, but he could hear a man speaking in English–something about examining merchandise–followed by laughter.

He and Cameron leaned closer, straining to listen, though a moment later, he wished he hadn't heard it.

The man was talking to someone he called Chase, saying something about how he liked latinas because they had 'some fight in them'. Clearly, he was talking about Lauren.

After that, the line went quiet again.

"I heard Lauren a minute ago," Ben said into his earpiece. "She's there for sure. Alive."

Reilly caught Cameron's eye.

"Unless the cartel had other accomplices waiting in the warehouse, it has to be those two nerdy-looking guys we heard," Reilly said finally. "More importantly, it doesn't sound like El Pez is with them."

If only she had an earpiece in, he'd be able to know for sure, but it was his best shot at an educated guess.

"Wonder where that snake has slithered off to," Cam said, shaking his head in disgust.

"I don't care any more," Reilly admitted. "The job was already shot. What I care about now is that he no longer has a knife to Lauren's neck, and she's with the two guys who pose the smallest physical threat."

That, too, was a guess–by the sound of what the man had said over the speakers, Reilly guessed that he was willing to commit sexual violence if given the chance–but nothing about the man or the younger one with him suggested they were hardened cartel members.

He'd take fighting the two of them over El Pez alone any day of the week.

"They're probably still armed," Cam pointed out.

"Look, Cam," Reilly said. "It's now or never if Lauren's going to have a chance. I need to go in."

Cameron's blue eyes met his, and for a second, he could hear nothing but the sound of their breathing in the cab of the truck.

"He's right, Cam," Ben said over the earpiece.

At last, his cousin nodded.

"Are you sure you want to do this? You're risking your life for an informant."

"As crazy as it sounds, I think God brought Lauren into

my life for a reason. I'm not about to let her get carried off by the cartel, whatever happens to me."

The fierceness of his own voice surprised him, but every word of what he said was true. In the short time they'd known each other, Lauren had found her way into his heart. He had to see where it would lead, if she would let him.

But first, they all had to get out of this alive.

"Do you need backup?" Cam asked, adjusting the gun holster at his belt.

Reilly shook his head.

"Call it in to El Paso PD, and be ready to gun it out of here as soon as we get back."

LAUREN

The sound of breaking glass somewhere outside the office shattered Lauren's thoughts.

A second later, she heard running feet, though she couldn't tell if it was more than one person or not.

As she glanced around, she felt the lawyer jabbing her in the shoulder with the barrel of the gun.

"Cops?" he asked her, not waiting for an answer before he turned to Chase and repeated his question.

The young lawyer said nothing, but moved away from the windows, coming to rest only a couple of feet away from where she now sat. His handsome face looked even paler than it had before, and his eyes were wide with fear.

Lauren tried to focus on breathing in and out, willing her racing heart to slow.

Could she dare to hope that it was the police?

Had Reilly and the team at FBS at least told someone what was going on before fleeing the scene?

She didn't want to allow herself to hope. Even if it was the cops, it didn't change the fact that she was a hostage, and a highly disposable one.

The footsteps in the hallway drew closer, and she could hear the sound of someone opening doors as they went.

"Keep your mouth shut," the lawyer kept saying in her ear, no longer giving even an inch of clearance between her and the gun. "Just keep your mouth shut."

She looked over at Chase, who was standing with his arms crossed over his chest, his eyes darting between the door and the windows behind them, as though unsure which part of the room was more dangerous to be in.

He wasn't armed.

She was certain that there was only one gun in this room, and the older lawyer was using it to keep her in line. If someone came in and he tried to use it on him, perhaps she could–

The door swung open without warning.

It wasn't the cops.

It was Reilly.

He held a much larger gun in his hands, and was pointing it directly at the lawyer's head.

"Drop it!" he barked, jabbing the barrel closer.

Lauren flinched, shrinking back from the weapon.

The lawyer lifted his hands, relieving the pressure against her neck and shoulder, but still, he didn't drop the weapon.

"Do you honestly think you're gonna beat me in a gunfight?" Reilly shouted at the top of his voice. "Drop the gun, now!"

The man let out what she could only describe as a whimper of defeat as he let the gun crash to the floor. Chase pulled back, narrowly avoiding the weapon landing directly on his shoes.

She stuck out a foot and kicked it toward Reilly, who was already stepping toward her, his gun still trained on the man as he knelt down to retrieve the firearm.

"You," he said to Chase, "get–"

The next moment happened between heartbeats.

The other door, the one that Lauren had thought was a closet, opened fast, banging against the wall.

El Pez was through it in a second, his own gun pointed directly at her face.

Time ceased moving as she heard shots.

One, two, three.

She closed her eyes and fell, her side slamming hard into the concrete floor below.

CHAPTER
EIGHTEEN

REILLY

Reilly looked down at the floor, watching as Lauren's chest rose and fell, but there was little relief.

He looked down at the still-warm gun in his hands.

On the floor beside her lay the younger man, who was bleeding out from a gunshot wound at the center of his chest.

It wasn't the result of a handgun round.

Somehow, when he'd aimed for El Pez, the man had gotten in the way.

It was his bullet that had caused the damage.

His fault.

He wanted to check if he was breathing, and to offer first aid, but decided against it. If he and Lauren weren't going to be victims themselves, he had to act fast.

The cartel boss was kneeling on the floor now, his rough hands scrabbling over the concrete, swearing all the while. He must have dropped the handgun he'd been using.

Reilly gripped his own compact assault rifle more tightly,

but he couldn't bring himself to shoot now that the man was temporarily disarmed.

They had a few seconds, and El Paso police and likely the DEA were on their way.

El Pez's arrest could lead to the downfall of the largest cartel in Juárez, but that required keeping him alive.

The older lawyer was sitting against a stack of boxes, looking dazed.

In any case, he was unarmed, and Reilly doubted he'd be up for giving chase.

He made a split-second decision.

"Get up, Lauren!" he shouted instead, stepping toward her as her eyes began blinking open.

El Pez was still swearing as he laid against the floor, reaching under a desk. If he found his weapon, Reilly would have no choice but to shoot again.

This time, he would hit his intended target.

He reached down and grabbed Lauren's arm.

To his relief, she was able to get to her feet. Dragging her forward, he yanked her through the open door of the office, slamming it behind them.

He heard only the rush of their desperate breathing as they ran side by side, Reilly turning every few seconds to point his gun the way they had come.

Somehow, Lauren seemed to know the way out, and he found himself following her lead as the sound of footsteps began to echo in the distance. El Pez was almost certainly on his way by now.

They rounded several corners, racing through the labyrinthine office space until Reilly had completely lost his sense of direction.

"In here," Lauren called out, breathless, gesturing toward one of the unmarked wooden doors. He opened it easily and the two of them rushed in.

To his relief, there were several windows, high along the

far wall. He could see the pitch blackness of the desert beyond.

There were more voices in the hall now, and more running feet.

It could be law enforcement, he supposed, but it could also be El Pez's goons.

He wasn't going to stick around long enough to find out.

"Come on!" he shouted, rushing over to the wall and glancing up at the windows. Lauren wasn't going to be able to get up there herself, and there was no time for arranging furniture.

Sending up a silent prayer for protection, he rested his gun against the side of a huge potted cactus and laced his fingers into a basket. "Hurry."

Lauren hesitated for less than a second before stepping onto his hands and reaching overhead. As she took hold of the edge of the windowsill, he boosted her up, his arms straining beneath her weight.

In a moment, she was there.

The window was unlocked.

She shoved the pane upward easily, and within a few seconds, she pulled her body through the narrow opening and disappeared.

Any sound that would indicate she'd landed safely was overtaken by the shouts and rushing footsteps in the hallways behind him.

He looked from the open window to his gun below.

It was too high to throw it through, and if he strapped it to his back, he doubted he'd fit.

"I'm trusting you, Jesus," he muttered under his breath, reaching his fingers up to the windowsill.

His muscles screamed once more as he dragged himself up, bracing one foot against the edge of a bookshelf. It was just enough leverage for him to get one elbow over the sill, and then another.

"Watch out!" he shouted into the darkness below.

"I'm here!" Lauren's voice sounded.

Relief flooded his chest as he dove through the window. There was no room to turn around. He ducked into a roll as he hit the hard-packed sand below, but the jolt to his shoulder upon landing was a small price to pay.

They were out.

Lauren was beside him in an instant, taking his hand and running beside him through the darkness.

He glanced around, trying desperately to get his bearings. It was dark here, far from the lamps in the makeshift court-yard area, and there were several buildings that looked pretty much identical. Even Lauren seemed lost.

He pulled his phone from his pocket and hit Cameron's name, turning on speakerphone as they continued to run through the shadows.

"Cam, where are–"

Gunshots rang out, and the phone slipped from his fingers, disappearing into the dark sand at their feet as they continued to run. There was no time to hunt for it.

They had made it only a few feet when more shots sounded.

Lauren grabbed his arm, hard, and the two of them tumbled to the dirt just as several more rounds struck the sand mere feet away, sending dust into their faces.

Two bright lights lit up the night as the sound of an old engine roared.

Somehow, Cam had found them.

They got to their feet and ran as fast as they could.

CHAPTER
NINETEEN

LAUREN

They reached the truck just as Cameron slammed on the brakes.

Lauren climbed into the cab, shoving a laptop onto the floor as Reilly clambered in behind her and shut the door with a bang.

He reached for her seatbelt and drew it over her waist. "Hold on," he said as she took the buckle from his hands, fumbling to click it into place as he strapped himself in.

"I need Cam's phone," he said. "Front pocket."

Lauren hesitated for a moment.

"No time to be shy," Cameron said, shoving his foot on the gas. The engine protested as the old truck lurched forward, hitting brush and rocks as he searched for the road.

More gunshots pierced the darkness.

Lauren reached toward his pocket and grabbed the phone, holding it out to Reilly, who took several attempts to hit the number he was looking for as they bumped and lurched over the off-road terrain.

Out the window, she watched as they passed one of the buildings, and then another.

She could hear a couple more gunshots, but they seemed to be passing out of the danger zone. Up ahead, she could see only sand in the glow of the headlights.

"We're fleeing the scene, Gabe," Reilly said, shouting to be heard over the wailing of the struggling engine. The vehicle made sense for surveillance, but it was probably the worst getaway car they could have possibly chosen. "Tell El Paso PD there's at least one casualty. Male, white, early twenties. GSW to the chest."

Reilly paused.

Lauren watched as he swiped at his eyes with the back of his free hand.

Realization dawned even before Reilly spoke again, the terrible, chaotic moment rushing into Lauren's mind with sudden clarity.

"I shot him, Gabe," he choked out. Even over the sounds of the truck bumping over the scrub below, she could hear the sob that escaped his throat. "It was an accident. He might still be alive, but he needs urgent medical care."

Through the other end of the phone, Lauren could hear the other man saying something, but she couldn't make out the words.

A few seconds later, Cam pulled onto what must have been a road, and the violent jolting and rattling of the truck stilled somewhat.

Reilly hung up Cam's phone, tossing it into the glove compartment and slamming it closed with a bang.

Everyone went silent as they raced into the desert.

Cam glanced over at Reilly, his face grave as he held the steering wheel with white knuckles, but Reilly only stared out at the dusty track that stretched out beyond their headlights.

Clearly, he had nothing to say, but when he placed his

head in his hands, Lauren reached out and rested a hand upon his shoulder.

He didn't shy away from her touch, and as they continued to drive, she began to feel a new emotion breaking through the guilt, heaviness, and sorrow that filled the cab of the old truck.

Hope.

Her desperate prayers had been heard, after all.

Even though it had meant risking death, Reilly hadn't abandoned her to the Iron Prophets and to the cartel.

He came back for her.

He'd saved her life.

CHAPTER
TWENTY

REILLY

The sound of distant sirens filled the air.

Reilly glanced over his shoulder, but he could see nothing but brief flashes of light as the vehicles rushed by in the distance behind them. Somewhere, another road led to the warehouse, but for the moment, he'd stopped caring about which route the police would take. He could only hope that however they got there, a well-equipped ambulance would be right behind them.

"Maybe they'll be able to confiscate some of the fentanyl," Cameron suggested from behind the wheel.

"Maybe," he said, glancing over at Lauren, who said nothing.

She was perched between him and his cousin, her body stiff and straight as she stared straight ahead through the windshield. She'd been through hell, and it showed on her face.

He didn't dare to ask if images of the young man's body were haunting her mind, too.

He looked down at his lap, offering a silent prayer that the kid was still alive, but he wasn't hopeful. There'd been a lot of blood.

Lauren lifted a hand, hovering near his shoulder as though she was going to reach out to comfort him again before pulling back a moment later.

He paused.

Cameron had been right about everything.

He'd been too close to this case from the moment he'd met Lauren, and his involvement had put all three of them at risk. It might have also been the reason that a young man was now dead.

He reached over and wrapped his arm around the woman's shoulder, pulling her closer until her head rested against his chest. His heart was pounding loud enough that even Cam could probably hear it, but he no longer cared.

Whatever mistakes he'd made, it was too late now to take any of them back. And right now, Lauren needed him.

Morning would come.

Gabe would have questions, as would the El Paso police and likely the DEA. After that, there'd be lawyers and court cases and unrelenting paperwork.

But for now, the terrible night was over, and even as the last of the adrenaline fled his body, he couldn't help but to feel the thrill of new possibilities that were opening up before him.

No matter how little time he had in his life for relationships, he couldn't deny how he felt about her.

And right now, she was here in his arms.

He had no intention of letting her go.

LAUREN

His heartbeat felt like home.

Lauren pressed her head more tightly against Reilly's chest, thankful to be able to shield her face from Cameron's view. He was close enough that she could feel his leg pressing against hers on her other side, but for the moment, he remained mercifully silent despite the awkwardness.

"It's going to be okay," Reilly said in a throaty whisper. "Just like I promised."

She shivered as his breath brushed against her ear.

Her heartbeat had slowed a little now that she was no longer fearing for her life, but the butterflies in her stomach had only grown more acrobatic the longer he held her.

She no longer noticed the poorly-paved road, or the whine of the old engine when Cameron accelerated.

The only thing she cared about was the warmth of Reilly's chest against her cheek. So long as it continued to rise and fall with his breaths, the darkness of the last several hours was possible to bear.

After what they'd just been through together, it was no surprise that she longed for the security his strong arms provided.

But could that really mean that he'd want more when the dawn came?

She couldn't think about it for long.

Cameron cleared his throat as he turned onto another, larger highway. This one had a properly painted yellow line in the middle, and an actual sign to indicate the distance to the nearest gas station.

"I'm just going to offer a quick prayer," Cam said. She felt Reilly nodding, but to her relief, he didn't pull his arms away from her.

"Our Lord Jesus Christ," Cameron began, "we pray for the survival and recovery of the young man who was shot tonight. We pray that if it is Your will for him to live, You will help to guide him aside from his present path to destruction and help him to find real meaning and purpose in his life. We pray also for the rest of the members of the cartel, as well as for the Iron Prophets, that they will repent of their evil deeds and seek You. Amen."

She felt Reilly dipping his head. "Amen."

"Amen," she added softly, the word surprising her even as it left her lips.

She meant it.

And there were many more things she wanted to add to Cameron's prayer.

Even after so many years of stubbornness and pride, maybe it wasn't too late. Maybe the sins she'd committed weren't so big that Jesus couldn't love her, too. Maybe her *abuelita* had been right all along. Maybe God not only forgave, but transformed, as well.

She closed her eyes and listened to the steady sound of Reilly's breathing.

Was it possible that tomorrow wouldn't be the end for the two of them?

That someone like him might actually take a chance on someone as broken as she was?

REILLY

The bright lights of El Paso felt strange and unsettling after spending time in the desert.

Reilly laid back against his seat, content to do nothing but keep watch over Lauren's sleeping form as Cameron navigated the twisting streets toward an address that Gabe had sent over.

He was too restless to sleep now, but he knew that as soon as he found a real bed, he'd be out for the count. He could only hope that law enforcement would hold off on their need for statements and interviews until after breakfast, and preferably several cups of coffee.

"That's it there, I think," Cameron's voice cut into his fantasies of steaming-hot French roast.

"Whew," Reilly breathed as they turned onto the street, slowing down as they passed several stately adobe-style homes. Their truck would stick out here, but hopefully it was late enough that most of the residents were already asleep and not waiting to call in the neighborhood watch. Grace would no doubt have someone come by and swap it with something more fitting by the time they woke the next morning, anyway.

Lauren lifted her head from his chest, combing through her brown hair with her fingers as he tried to discreetly shake out the damp sweat from his shirt before she noticed it.

"Where are we?" she asked, pausing to give a huge yawn.

"This is one of our network's safehouses," Cam explained. "We'll all stay here for the next few days while we work with the police and the DEA. Just as a precaution."

"Then what?" Lauren asked.

"Reilly will talk to you about that," his cousin said, giving him a pointed look.

Lauren said nothing, and a couple minutes later they were getting out of the car and heading up to the huge metal gate.

Cameron tapped a few buttons on a keypad, and after a loud buzz, the gate swung inward.

Reilly took Lauren's hand and led her forward until they'd reached the foyer. The house was huge and well-decorated, and despite the late hour, there was a woman in a housekeeper's uniform making sandwiches in the kitchen.

"Hi there," Cameron called out. The woman turned and waved hello, saying nothing before she returned to her task.

"Can't say this is what I expected a safehouse to be like," Lauren said, staring as she took everything in.

"Grace really is a miracle worker," Reilly said.

There was an awkward pause.

"I'm gonna go lay down," Cam said, clearing his throat. "I'll see you guys at dawn."

"I can bring you over a sandwich when they're done," the

housekeeper called out, her voice cheerful. "I'll just be a minute."

"That would be awesome, thank you so much," Cam said.

Without another word, he disappeared down one of the several hallways that led into the depths of the house, the sound of his footsteps fading into silence.

"Let's sit," Reilly suggested, pointing toward a living area toward the back of the house. Through a huge picture window, he could see the gleaming blue of a lit swimming pool. Despite the high walls and, presumably, patrolling security, he always felt safer when he could see outside.

As they sat down on two soft armchairs, the silence continued to settle on them, broken only by the housekeeper humming across the house.

"So," Lauren said. "I want to know. What happens next?"

The beating of Reilly's heart felt heavy in his chest as he contemplated what to say. He wanted nothing more than to reach out and hold her again, but it was clear that the moment had passed. Lauren looked wide awake, and she deserved answers.

"You can't live in El Paso anymore, or anywhere near it," he said carefully. "If you want to leave the Iron Prophets, you need to start over completely."

Lauren didn't look surprised as she nodded.

"San Antonio is where Forge Brothers Security is head-quartered," he said. "It's where we can best protect you."

Lauren leaned toward him a little in her chair, her dark eyes difficult to read in the dim light. He knew she'd have a million questions, but for now, there was one he'd happily answer before she asked.

"It's also where I live," he added, ignoring the fresh pangs of anxiety that were rippling through him. "I want to keep getting to know you, Lauren Ortega. I hope you'll consider making space for me in your new life."

She drew back slightly, just enough that he felt himself flinch.

Was she rejecting him?

Maybe he'd misinterpreted her feelings all along. High-adrenaline situations had a way of clouding minds. Perhaps it was all business for her, now that the danger had passed.

He glanced over at her, and the stream of thoughts calmed at once when he noticed that her eyes were filled with tears.

"I'm so broken, you know?" she said, her voice barely breaking a whisper. "I've been a mess my entire life. I have no skills at anything that doesn't involve slinging dope. I have nothing to offer. Reilly, you deserve someone better. You deserve someone who—"

Reilly got out of his chair so fast that it scraped against the tile floor.

He couldn't hear her talk about herself that way for a single second longer.

He reached down and took her hands in his own, pulling her to her feet until he was looking down at her, her flawless face mere inches from his own.

After the growth and the courage she'd shown, that was what she was worried about? That she wasn't good enough?

He shook his head as she tried to speak again, placing a gentle finger over her lips.

There was so much he wanted to say to her, so many points that he wanted to make.

He would, eventually.

No matter how many days, weeks, or months it took, he'd make her see that he wanted her.

And, more importantly, that God wanted her.

But for now, he was too tired to argue.

He pulled his finger away and smiled down at her, grasping her waist with his free hand and drawing her in as close as he could.

Her eyes met his, and he knew that what she needed most could not be explained in words.

He leaned down and pressed his lips against hers, hoping that the sun would not rise for a long, long time.

Until then, he would kiss her until she knew.

She was safe.

And she was loved.

EPILOGUE

CAMERON

The only thing missing was the snow.

Cameron glanced over the balcony of his hotel room at the atrium below, where the biggest Christmas tree he'd ever seen stood sentinel over the mingling wedding guests.

He had just finished getting dressed in his suit, and was now waiting for the rest of the wedding party to get themselves in order.

The men, anyway. He didn't even want to know how long the ladies would take to get dressed and perfect their hair and makeup.

Before he could consider finding a cup of coffee to tide him over until the reception, however, his father, his cousin, and his brothers poured out of the room behind him and joined him at the wooden railing.

"Careful that Lauren doesn't see you," Cameron teased Reilly, looking the groom over as he adjusted his tie for the millionth time.

"Superstitious nonsense," his father grumbled.

"True," Gabe Jr. chimed in, "but I guarantee you she's still in her room, probably imprisoned in a makeup chair with five people working on her. I know how these things go."

Ben and Asher gave each other a knowing glance, and Cameron suppressed a smile. Like the rest of his brothers, Gabe was still unmarried, much to their father's chagrin. Most of his wedding knowledge had been gained by watching reality television, not that he'd ever admit to his habit.

Still, he was glad that his dad and oldest brother seemed to be getting along better than usual for the sake of Reilly and Lauren's big day.

"It really is a nice venue," Gabe Sr. said, gesturing toward one of the hundreds of strands of warm Christmas lights that had been hung up around the lodge. "I can almost forget I'm in Texas."

"Now that would be a sight to see," Asher joked. "When's the last time you left the Lone Star state, pops?"

"It wasn't that long ago," Gabe Sr. retorted. "Your mother and I went up to Alaska that time, remember?"

"To be fair, I'm not sure Asher and I remember much about events that took place prior to the fall of the Berlin Wall," Ben added with a wink. "Seeing as we weren't actually born yet."

"All right, all right," Reilly cut in. "If you clowns are ready, I'd appreciate it if you could go down there and start urging the guests to walk toward the church."

Gabe Jr. nodded and gestured toward the stairs, ushering for their father to lead the way.

Cameron moved to follow, but Reilly placed a restraining hand on the arm of his suit jacket before he could.

"I just need a minute with my best man," he explained.

The two of them watched as the others headed out onto the ground floor below, all smiles as they mingled with the guests.

There were at least two hundred, the vast majority of them coming from Reilly's side, though a few of Lauren's friends had made it from El Paso for the big event.

Cam could also see Lauren's grandmother sitting in a wheelchair near one of the enormous lit fireplaces, beaming at everyone who greeted her, though he'd learned from his own embarrassing experience that the sweet woman hardly spoke a word of English.

"I wish Jacob was here," Reilly said after a moment. "It's been years since all of us have actually been under the same roof."

"Did you get to talk to him about what's happening, at least?" Cameron asked. He wasn't terribly optimistic about his cousin's answer. Jacob was currently aiding a rural village mission in Mauritania, and his access to electricity was limited.

To make matters more difficult, the country was not friendly to Christians, and especially not to those who sought to preach Jesus Christ to their majority-Muslim population.

To his surprise, Reilly nodded. "I did, actually. Two weeks ago. He had business in the capital and wanted to check in with us. I don't think he was expecting me to tell him I was getting married."

Cameron laughed. "I highly doubt it."

Reilly said nothing, and the two men lapsed into silence again, watching as a few more stragglers headed out of the lodge.

The place felt even more cozy without the crowd, and Cameron found himself wishing for a book and some Christmas cookies next to a raging fire rather than a party that would probably continue late into the night.

"So, are you ready to head out? I don't want Lauren beating us there and thinking that you left her at the altar."

Cam tried to keep his tone light, but Reilly's expression remained unreadable.

"Do you think this is crazy?" his cousin asked, fiddling with his tie once more. "Marrying a woman four months after meeting her?"

Cameron considered this.

Finally, he nodded.

"Lauren's not just any woman, Reilly. She's an ex gang member and drug mule who just started coming back to church. Sounds like a recipe for marital bliss to me."

Reilly's mouth fell open.

"I'm joking!" Cameron cut in, shaking his head. "Bro, come on. You really think that I wouldn't have said anything by now if I was worried?"

"I mean, that's true. None of you have. Not even uncle Gabe."

"Or other Gabe," Cam pointed out. "If he didn't like her, you wouldn't have heard the end of it."

"That's true."

Reilly's shoulders relaxed slightly.

"Sometimes you just know," Cameron said firmly. "Lauren has a good heart, and we can all see it. She's been through a lot, and that's going to bring challenges to your marriage, but I really do believe that God brought her into your life for a reason. And part of that reason is for you to build a home and a life with her. A future."

He paused, glancing over at his cousin. The color seemed to be returning to his face, so he pressed on.

"We know that marriage is impossible on our own. None of us can be loving enough, or strong enough, or patient enough. But with God's grace, it becomes a gift. It becomes a challenge that can be met."

"I love her so much," Reilly said after a moment. Cameron could see tears glistening at the edges of the man's eyes. He didn't doubt it for a second–and by the way Lauren always looked at his cousin, he knew that she felt the exact same way. "You're right. It is crazy, but I'm going to step out in faith and make my vows. I'm not going to be good enough. I just have to trust that God will make up for what I'm missing."

Cameron clapped his cousin on the back. Leave it to Reilly to doubt his worth. Even after all the huge mistakes Lauren had made in her life, he still felt like he was the one who was going to mess it all up.

"So how about you?" Reilly asked, raising an eyebrow. "Are you open to God bringing a new woman into your future?"

"Sure," Cam said quickly. "If it's the right person."

Reilly rolled his eyes. "If you say so."

"All right, let's go," Cameron said, taking the first couple of steps down the large wooden staircase.

To his relief, Reilly fell in beside him, letting the matter rest for now.

Not that he could blame his cousin for being skeptical.

Even after so many years had passed, there was still one woman that Cameron could never quite seem to get out of his head.

Or his heart.

———

Thank you for reading *Forged in Darkness*, a Forge Brothers Security prequel novella.

I can't wait to share Cameron's story with you in *Forged in Peril*, coming spring 2024!

FORGED IN PERIL

She can't keep running...

Ambitious paralegal Bristol Chaplin knows that achieving her dream of becoming a lawyer won't be easy, but there's a price that even she isn't willing to pay. When a dark secret threatens to destroy her career, she's forced to seek help from the man she thought she'd left behind forever.

Private security operative Cameron Forge is content to spend his life serving God and protecting the innocent. But as the woman who broke his heart brings danger straight to his doorstep, he realizes that keeping her safe might be his toughest mission yet.

With hidden threats lurking behind every shadow, they have no choice but to uncover the truth about who is hunting Bristol before it's too late. Even if it means putting their lives—and hearts—on the line.

Serve. Protect. Redeem.

ABOUT THE AUTHOR

Kendra Warden lives in Ontario, Canada, with her husband, three young children, two cats, and a whole lot of books. She's passionate about (very) early mornings, long walks, and buffalo sauce. She loves to write exciting suspense stories that encourage readers to trust in the protection and love of Jesus.

https://www.kendrawarden.com

Made in the USA
Columbia, SC
03 June 2024

36568864R00090